CW00589816

G R JORDAN

Ship of Doom

First published by Carpetless Publishing 2019

Copyright © 2019 by G R Jordan

All rights reserved. No part of this publication may be reproduced, stored or transmitted in any form or by any means, electronic, mechanical, photocopying, recording, scanning, or otherwise without written permission from the publisher. It is illegal to copy this book, post it to a website, or distribute it by any other means without permission.

This novel is entirely a work of fiction. The names, characters and incidents portrayed in it are the work of the author's imagination. Any resemblance to actual persons, living or dead, events or localities is entirely coincidental.

G R Jordan asserts the moral right to be identified as the author of this work.

G R Jordan has no responsibility for the persistence or accuracy of URLs for external or third-party Internet Websites referred to in this publication and does not guarantee that any content on such Websites is, or will remain, accurate or appropriate.

Designations used by companies to distinguish their products are often claimed as trademarks. All brand names and product names used in this book and on its cover are trade names, service marks, trademarks and registered trademarks of their respective owners. The publishers and the book are not associated with any product or vendor mentioned in this book. None of the companies referenced within the book have endorsed the book.

First edition

ISBN: 978-1-912153-39-8

Cover art by J Caleb Clarke

*This book was professionally typeset on Reedsy.
Find out more at reedsy.com*

To Zach and Toby, and our imagined battles.

Contents

Acknowledgement

As always, first and foremost to Janet and my family for giving me the time and space to dream these strange worlds and bring them to fruition.

To my readers, for taking the time to read my stories, I hope you find them worthwhile.

To Jake for the stunning covers, for bringing the dreams to life.

To Roma for the edit and encouragement.

To those who support me with reviews, social media posts and comments and everything else in this writing life.

1

Prologue

In its six-month life, the coffee shack had grown from its humble beginnings. After a poor customer count of six on its opening day, it was now a place to be seen, a place that spoke of premium smells and wafts of various coffees, and a range of peculiar ice varieties of tea and the dark bean. "The Dark Bean" had been an inspired choice for a name, and now it was spoken of on the island as a top destination on an evening out.

The clientele were usually dressed in shorts and t-shirts or some other up-to-date, colourful garb that Andrew had never seen as an aid to a happier one. They were like the colourful birds that were seen on the island, all show and not so much tell. Occasionally some would depart with each other only to return the following week trying to leave with a different "bird". But they paid the bills, and a lot more these days, and so Andrew entertained their ridiculous requests for the blaspheming of his coffee.

All of this made what he saw now so bizarre. There was a man of moderate stature, trim and lean, dressed like he had come from the London Stock exchange in his pinstripe suit and bowler hat. On entering, he had made straight for a table that had at least twenty people around it, one of whom had two women on either side wearing so very little that Andrew wondered if they were about to shower. But these women were flanked by men with arms like tree trunks and weapons that stuck out of their jackets.

To date, "The Dark Bean" had never witnessed any real trouble. Once it had gotten quite heated between rival gang lords, but they had taken it outside as there was an unwritten rule about this sort of meeting place. If you kept it so well that it hurt to dirty it, they generally didn't. This stranger, however, didn't seem to be aware of the rule.

The first hulk of a man stepped forward in a large Hawaiian shirt and was promptly forced to double over as an umbrella point was drilled into his stomach. The stranger then grabbed the apparent bodyguard's hair and sent him spiralling backwards with what seemed to be a flick of his wrist. Two more giants stepped forward and were broken down at speed, despatched to a far off wall, clattering through tables as customers scattered.

Andrew thought about interjecting but then remembered how much he loved life and the fact that recent takings meant he could probably cover this damage.

A gun was pulled on the stranger and as it was fired it seemed to turn back towards the shooter and he fell for the last time as the scene become distinctly bloodier. More guns were drawn and were removed from strong hands like they were items made from butter. The two women flanking the head of the party now shrunk in fear but the stranger reached out with both his hands, pulling the women up and letting them depart.

Andrew overheard the polite English voice that said, "Ladies" before the gang leader was picked up and driven onto a table.

How an umbrella could be considered a weapon, Andrew wasn't sure, but he was certain that this particular umbrella was definitely a weapon and that it seemed more deadly than a gun. Its tip was jarred into the stricken man's throat and the stranger looked over at Andrew.

"My apologies, my good man, but I seem to have caused some damage. I regret that this action had to take place but these men have something I'm looking for. Of course, I shall recompense you for the damage but for now can I be so bold as to ask if you have any tea available? Earl Grey, perhaps? Or Darjeeling if not. Thank you, kind sir, I'll just carry on here while you get that. I doubt one will be long."

His hands reaching for the Darjeeling, Andrew continued to watch the stranger as he focused back on his target and pushed the umbrella tip further into the man's throat but without breaking the surface.

"I have travelled to places that you will never see, and frankly, I don't really care about what you do or don't do here. What I want to know is, where is he?"

The man being asked the question had two hands on the umbrella, desperately trying to force it away from his throat, but he also had a look of fear. A fear borne of something other than his current situation.

"You think that he will come for you, that he can hurt you...badly. Be aware, I am more skilled than he in these arts. And I will hurt you. Where did he go?"

The man struggled, tears forming in his eyes and he croaked out something. The umbrella was lifted slightly. "Kindly repeat as I believe that you somewhat gargled that."

"Barko Ng Tadhana."

"Really? How apt! Is the tea ready, my dear proprietor?"

Andrew rushed over with a cup of Darjeeling, produced almost blindly by his hands as he watched. He set it down on the table beside the stricken man.

"My sincerest thanks and apologies for the disturbance." The stranger turned and raised the cup to his lips, taking a small sip. "Very good, sir. For where we are, rather surprising actually. But now I must go."

Andrew watched as the man turned on his heel and walked calmly and elegantly out of the door. The coffee house was almost deserted except for the bodies, littered around the stranger's original path. But on the wind he heard a mutter under the breath from the stranger. Just six words. *Barko Ng Tadhana—Ship of Doom.*

2

Boarding

As he emerged from the taxi, Kirkgordon took a deep breath of sea air. He was not a natural mariner but the cruise ship he was looking at was no normal sea vessel. It was like someone had grabbed three or four hotels and shoved them on top of a cargo vessel's hull and then gone to work with a most exquisite paint job. Yes, this would be proper sailing. He was almost looking forward to it, despite having Austerley in tow.

With his new foot now fully settled in, Austerley was back to almost complete fitness, or as close as he ever got to the word *fit*. The shambling hulk of a man clambered out of the other side of the taxi and grimaced at the enormous vessel before them on the dock. Kirkgordon noticed a hesitancy in Austerley he was not used to, especially when they were off to investigate the weird.

And weird was what it was. Wilson had given further briefings after their audience with Ma'am and had Austerley licking his lips. Apparently, a gentleman of English descent had been spending a lot of time in Haiti and speaking to various nefarious characters, learning the secrets of voodoo, and a particular strand that was unknown to Austerley. Indeed, Austerley corrected Wilson in that it was more of a cult than a strand, not a different systematic approach but more a different use. Either way, they were to investigate this individual who was taking a cruise at this time, a cruise that was due to pass through the Bermuda triangle.

Watching the taxi driver pass their luggage to some porters, Kirkgordon marvelled at Austerley's three suitcases, compared to his single valise. Gone were the bow and arrows. These days he was carrying his armoury inside his prosthetic hand and arm. Having been damaged during his rescue of Calandra in the "Nether Lands", he was still in wonder at the new hand and arm combination he had been given. At a thought, his arm would open up and produce a small crossbow, complete with a bolt supply, with which to target enemies. And yet to look at his fake skin, you would never guess it was anything other than a normal arm. And the feeling from the prosthetic was almost perfect. Almost.

A glimpse of bright colour from Austerley's direction caused Kirkgordon to look at his colleague who had removed the standard duffel coat he usually wore. Underneath he was sporting a vivid Hawaiian shirt with deep blues, sunlight yellows and arrangements of palm trees and surf boards. It railed against the camouflage trousers and dark black boots.

"What the hell is that?" asked Kirkgordon, standing in black trousers and leather jacket.

"We are going undercover. I see you have made no effort." Austerley stood and shook his head.

"Undercover? You couldn't look any more like you were trying to blend in. Why is it you make an arse out of

6

everything?"

"Sorry, Mister Look-at-me-I'm-James-Bond-in-my-subtle-leather-disguise."

Kirkgordon tutted. "And why all the cases? I thought you could store stuff in your foot."

"My foot is a prosthetic for me to walk with, not an extra cargo hold. Besides, you can't shrink books into such a space. Not these books."

"Ever think of a tablet? You know that most people have one. You can get thousands of books on those. But then I guess you don't get yours online."

Kirkgordon watched Austerley's dirty glare before deciding enough was enough and they should get on board. As he made his way across the quayside, a car, black and powerful, raced along the dockside. As it hammered along, Kirkgordon thought he saw its destination, a white box painted on the quayside across which his valise and Austerley's epic baggage were being carried. And the car wasn't for stopping. He ran.

The car entered the white box just as Kirkgordon threw himself at the porter who was last in the baggage train and still inside the box. As he hit the ground, clear of the box and on top of the porter, he smelt the rubber that had been forsaken to stop the vehicle. Standing, he turned to round on the driver. A rear door opened and a giant of a man stepped out. He was deeply tanned, possibly Mediterranean, and built like the proverbial brick house.

"You could have killed that man!" raged Kirkgordon. Turning around to point at the affected party, Kirkgordon saw him running with his luggage towards the ship. *Well, thanks.*

"Is there a problem?"

The voice came from the other side of the car, where a woman had stepped out of the front passenger seat. Tall and elegant with incredibly dark skin, she wore a mishmash of rags that somehow combined to look perfectly reasonable and that also showed an alluringly copious amount of flesh.

"Your driver nearly killed that man."

"I don't see anyone complaining. I would be most appreciative if you would clear the way and let Dr Howard board."

Before Kirkgordon could answer, a horde of porters and other staff were arriving, including a driver of a small buggy. A tall gentleman then emerged in a white suit from the car and climbed into the buggy without ever looking at Kirkgordon. Once the dark skinned woman was on board, the buggy sped off towards a gangway to the ship that wasn't being used by anyone else.

"That him?" It was Austerley.

"You got briefed the same as me. Of course it's him."

"He's packing a lot of protection."

"Oh, I could take that big guy."

"I was referring to the woman. I don't think you ever see past the chest and legs."

Kirkgordon went to argue but recent escapades said that Austerley was right. And then he thought of Alana. They said she was still crying out through the night. Still throwing herself off the walls of that padded cell. The darkness that had inflicted her from Dagon wasn't giving up its hold, and he didn't know if he'd ever see the woman he had first loved again.

He had gone to visit her, accompanied by Austerley, though not wanted. Wilson had insisted, worried about what might come out of Alana, what might stir when she saw the man who had ignored her wishes and ran off to save the other woman. Well, what could he have done, left Calandra to her fate? Left Austerley, who had risked everything to save Alana? No, that wasn't him. Whenever the siren went off for the needy and those in danger, he answered it. He was born to it.

She had been quiet, distant, to the point that they actually let her accompany him to the canteen area. There had been a word from her, two in fact. The names of their children. Children who had hit him and shouted at him when he didn't bring Mum home. And then when he had said about the kids, about how they were, she had become fierce. Calandra's name was mentioned, and as Kirkgordon had tried to say she had moved on, an arm had been swung at him sending him across the canteen, through the serving hatch and into some stainless steel tables. He was still feeling the bruising. Thankfully, Austerley had calmed her down with some type of low level chanting and she was returned to her padded cell.

Back to the matter in hand, though. He needed to get on board and establish the lay of the land around Dr Howard. The sooner this matter was resolved, the sooner he could get back to his kids.

Austerley had now lumbered over to a gangway and was gingerly making his way up the steep incline. The loud shirt was tightly stretched across his shoulders but hung limp elsewhere around his girth. Bounding up behind him, and thanking Wilson for booking them on the upper class of the passenger choices, Kirkgordon urged Austerley to speed up.

"Wait until you see this place inside. There's a massive interior hallway that has every sort of boutique, coffee house, restaurant and entertainment you want. There's even a library for you."

"Library, my arse. I doubt there's going to be any sort of book I would care to delve into."

Kirkgordon nodded. *Fair comment.* "But there's a wave board, cinema under the stars, casino—I mean, when have you ever been on something like this?"

"Twenty years ago. Bloody miserable hunk of junk."

Kirkgordon thought about pressing him about this but then thought better of it. There may be a sinister element to this trip, he may have a messed up home life, but at least in the here and now he could have a bit of fun.

Stepping through the small discreet entrance used by the ship's more elite guests, he was handed a flute of champagne and had a garland placed around his neck. As he glanced around the exquisite entrance hall with what looked like some expensive crystal and paintings, he heard a slight kerfuffle behind him.

"I'm not wearing some sort of flower band around my neck. No. There's head hunting tribes that wear this sort of nonsense."

"Austerley, stop making a scene," Kirkgordon said over his shoulder, and smiling at a pretty girl in island dress who was placing another garland over his head.

The pair were directed towards an immaculately dressed man with significant gold braiding on his shoulder who briefly checked their passports before issuing an order to a nearby crew member to show the men to their suite. Passing through to a smart if simple corridor, Kirkgordon thought how soundlessly Austerley walked with his prosthetic compared to how he had hobbled in the "Nether lands" with only a stump and wooden replacement. He was almost normal again. Kirkgordon cursed himself for using the word "normal". Just because someone had a missing limb didn't mean they weren't normal. Unlike Austerley. He wasn't normal.

As they made their way along, they joined a deck of the ship that didn't have corridors with a lot of doors. Kirkgordon assumed they were now amongst the suites and that their own must be close. A door opened behind him and he heard Austerley fall to the floor and then heard the cry of a woman. Turning around, he saw Austerley on his back and a tall, pale woman lying on top of him in a white robe bearing the insignia of the ship's company.

"Dammit woman, what do you…"

"Austerley, don't be so rude," hurried Kirkgordon, offering the woman a hand. As she rose, her legs were exposed and the pale, milky-white flesh of a perfect thigh caught Kirkgordon's eye.

On standing up, she was at least six inches taller than Kirkgordon and cut a stunning figure. "Enchanté, Monsieur," the woman said in what seemed like perfect French to Kirkgordon, before walking off in the direction they had come from. He watched her long legs disappearing around a distant corner.

"It's okay to give me a damn hand too."

"Get up. I think I'm beginning to enjoy travelling in this class," said Kirkgordon, smiling at the now empty corridor.

"Aye, if you really want to travel with vampires."

3

Sam

"What do you mean, vampires?"

The guide had just left the suite after being hurried through instructions and ship formalities by Kirkgordon, who was now rounding on Austerley as he delved into the mini bar.

"The things that suck your blood. Popularised by those sixties movies, staring eyes, turn into bats, like the odd virgin if you believe the hype." Taking two small bottles of whiskey, Austerley broke the seals and dropped them into a crystal tumbler.

"She was a vampire? You're telling me, she was a vampire and just happens to fall into your lap?"

"I do have a way with ladies of the night."

Kirkgordon shook his head. That sounded wrong on so many levels.

"We're on a cruise ship. A bloody cruise ship and you manage to find a vampire on a cruise ship?"

"Like I said…"

"No!" yelled Kirkgordon. "Stop right there. Stop making it

sound normal. It's not! Why would a vampire be on this ship? And in daylight?"

Austerley laughed. "What daylight? Here below decks there's no daylight. All artificial light. Doesn't affect them. And besides, she was quite high up the chain. Maybe royal."

"Royal? What the hell do you mean, royal?"

With the look of someone talking to a child, Austerley continued. "You know that they have hives. All with leaders and orders, similar to bees really. Different roles and tasks."

Kirkgordon's blank expression didn't change.

"Well they do. But she was from the top, cream of the crop. Wouldn't surprise me if she was a queen. Magnificent specimen."

"But why here?"

"Sometimes they move around. Can get a bit obvious if there's a lot of people with a total loss of blood." Austerley downed his whiskey and disappeared into his room.

The suite that Wilson had booked for them had 2 bedrooms, an open area with a sofa, television, computer terminal and a balcony giving a stunning view of the present harbour. Following Austerley into his room, Kirkgordon pressed him into further information.

"Is she a danger?"

"Hell, they are always dangerous. Also depends how many of them there are. And if they have supplies."

"Supplies?"

"Yes, they do need to feed. Or rest in the soil. I wonder if they have coffins on board."

"I'm sure we can take on a few of them."

Austerley nodded and began taking off his loud Hawaiian shirt. "If that's all there are."

13

"How many are you expecting?"

"Well, hives can be over a thousand strong but that would be a heck of a move." A new Hawaiian shirt, in bright reds and pinks was now on Austerley's shoulders and he topped it off with a straw hat.

Shaking his head, Kirkgordon turned away. "Anyway, we have other things to look at. Once we get underway, we need to clock Dr Howard's suite. Find out what he's up to. For now, we should explore the ship and work out the lay of the land."

Holding his arm out, Kirkgordon watched his forearm open up and a small pre-loaded crossbow emerged. "Armour!" The bolt changed and had a much bigger head on it. "Rope!" Again the bolt changed and became a small grappling hook in shape. "Fire!" The bolt changed again before the head erupted in flame. "Sweet," said Kirkgordon, watching it burn. "Losing my arm certainly had some compensations."

A shrill alarm sounded within the cabin, followed by a speaker asking everyone to vacate the deck.

"Churchy! That's the fire alarm, you clown. And you say my shorts are giving us away."

*****

About an hour later, Kirkgordon entered the main promenade of the ship. After the excitement of a quick evacuation of the deck and having to lie through his teeth about why the alarms had gone off, he needed a walk. Austerley had gone up to the uppermost deck to get fresh air apparently, but Kirkgordon reckoned he was just looking for space.

The promenade was amazing. The Calsten shipping company may have been one of the newer cruising companies but they had amazing vessels. This Calsten Universe, as the vessel was named, was decadent in the extreme. There were glass elevators and sweeping lines of gold and silver, statues and paintings, and a grand piano at which a rather talented pianist was playing something Kirkgordon reckoned he couldn't play with ten hands, never mind two.

He walked past a jewellery shop with prices that made his eyes water and a clothing shop complete with sailing sweaters and pinstripe trousers and plimsolls that were beyond his monthly pay. *How the other half bloody live.*

A coffee shop at the end of the promenade caught his eye, and as all drinks were free on board—well, soft drinks anyway—he made for it. Sitting down with a Kenyan blend black coffee, he was able to watch the bustling promenade, trying to clock anyone suspicious looking, or a creature that might be hunting for blood. *Vampires. I mean, vampires, it's always something with Austerley.*

"Hi."

Kirkgordon turned and saw a woman in jeans and a t-shirt looking a little out of place. "Hi."

"Do you mind if I sit down?"

He never considered himself someone who had a particular type of woman, but if he did, and yes, he knew he did, she may just fit the bill. The woman's blonde hair was falling in waves past her shoulders and she was fairly curvy. *What the hell, why not?"*

"Sure." Kirkgordon noticed that there were enough empty tables that the woman could sit alone if she wanted to.

"Thanks."

"You may want a coffee. Can I get you one?"

"Oh, right. Yes, coffee."

Kirkgordon watched her sit and a hand went to her hair,

preening it. *Ah, she's interested then. Should be careful, not give her any encouragement.* "Any particular kind?"

"Of what?"

She's totally distracted. Preening and yet distracted. At least she's got too much colour to be a vampire. "Coffee. What kind of coffee?"

"Any's fine."

"Any it is then." Kirkgordon walked to the serving desk and asked for a black coffee. If it was wrong, at least he could have it.

"There we go. Is that alright for you…?"

"Yes. Thanks."

Kirkgordon sat down beside the woman, and looked along the promenade to see if she was looking at anything in particular. Turning back, he saw the mark of a wedding ring on her hand but there was no jewellery on it.

"What's your name?"

"Sorry?"

"Can I ask your name?"

"Sorry. It's Sam. Short for Samantha."

"Kirkgordon. Nice to meet you, Sam. When did he leave and why are you here?"

The woman started at the question and then gave a little chuckle. "Oh, you got it all wrong. He didn't leave."

"There's no ring where there should be. You're distant and yet you seem to want company. You're touching your hair in a sort of subconscious flirt. Sorry to pry, but there is a story, but if you don't want to talk about it then just tell me to shut up."

The woman laughed again, slightly hollow, like the joke was only leading into a deep thought. "Well I did impose on you, I guess. But you're wrong. She left. And this is my getting away from it. And you seemed so at ease. Sorry."

"Ah…sorry. I guess I just assumed. Sorry, it is a new day. Old gits like me have to get more with today's way of things. Not that there's anything wrong with… Sorry I'll shut up. I couldn't really have put that any worse, could I?"

"Honestly, no. But it's okay. I've had a lot worse than some guy checking me out and then being surprised. Besides, I like both."

"Ah… okay, good to know. "

"I think we should really talk about something else," said Sam, "What about you?"

"Well, my wife's demented, possessed really, by contact with some sort of space alien from another dimension, while the other woman on my heart burnt me with ice last time I was saving her life. And I babysit the most dangerous man in the world. But my kids are normal. Well, normal enough considering their parents."

Sam laughed, a little nervously but with eyes that lit up at Kirkgordon. "And you are on a cruise, why?"

"Just keeping the vampires in check."

Kirkgordon watched her laugh again and noticed a kindness in her eyes that seemed a little bit broken.

"So you're not on holiday?"

"My whole life is a holiday or a weird sort of movie anyway."

"You seem like you need some fun company, and I sure as hell do, so what say we spend some time at the bar together?" Smiling like it was going out of fashion, Sam was leaning forward with a hand touching Kirkgordon's arm.

"Sure. No promises, no regrets, just drinks and a bit of banter. Will that do you?"

"Probably not, and maybe not you either, but if that's where we both are then, sure. Drinking buddies."

"Here's to plenty of coffees," said Kirkgordon. He watched her laugh again. She flirted like Alana did, back in the day. "Room 5835. It's a single occupancy. Knock me up."

"Okay. But you could have phrased that better."

"I didn't…" And he stared at her disappearing into the crowd on the promenade, coffee not even touched on the table. She was so like Alana. *Blonde but like Alana. Is she a spy, a rogue element, or just a lost soul like myself? I hope she's just lonely, I really do.*

4

Austerley, Pool Attendant

S taring at the wide range of bottles behind the bar, Austerley fought to make up his mind about the list ringing around his head of cocktails available. Names such as Funky Monkey, Sex on the Beach, Trojan Horse and Barking Spider raced through his consciousness but one thing was for sure, he wasn't about to have the Dragon's Breath.

It was good to know that Farthington, the shapeshifting dragon, was gone. Disappeared off a high platform above an abyss that led to the black void occupied by Dagon, and over which Austerley had swung for far too long. Although he now had his prosthetic, the memory of the dragon ripping his appendage off at the ankle still kept him awake at nights. But Havers had seen fit to launch himself into Farthington and take them both to their doom. Pity about Havers mind, although, he was never to be fully trusted. Too eager to remove appendages himself.

"Barking Spider, if you don't mind." Truth was that Austerley was in a good place. Having repaid any debts to Kirkgordon by saving his wife, he felt on an equal footing with his work companion, even if the other never acknowledged it. And here he was, looking out a window high up on the ship, drinking beverages containing whatever, and looking fairly normal in his straw hat and loud shirt and shorts. Yes, he felt good. In fact, almost normal.

Stretching his legs with drink in hand, Austerley wandered amongst the pool areas on the top decks, casually glancing at the array of bodies soaking up the day's sun. Pausing in what he hoped wasn't too obvious a fashion close to some rather attractive females, he was in buoyant form. So much so that he decided to take a deck chair under a parasol beside a private pool reserved for the higher class travellers.

A mature but elegant woman began swimming up and down the length of the pool, and Austerley slipped off his deck shoes and sat at the edge, dangling his feet into the cool water. As she turned at the end of the length she was completing, the mature woman cast Austerley a provocative smile and he felt somewhat flushed. But then a woman of African descent, extremely dark in skin tone, entered the pool at the far end. Her hair was short cropped and her figure was heavily toned, almost muscular, easily studied due to the skimpiness of her bikini. But Austerley wasn't looking at her flesh.

On her thigh he had spotted a symbol, one that intrigued him. A trident, raised high by a hand which had seaweed wrapped around it and flowing from it. He hadn't seen that symbol in years and even then it was just a legend. And on an African woman, that was strange. But then again they weren't far from that place, the doom of so many. Austerley had a very clear view about the Bermuda Triangle. Something was there, something took people and ships and aircraft. But he didn't know what that something was. Not yet.

The trident symbol had come up when he was perusing articles on islands that appeared and disappeared over time. There had been a woman in the background of a photograph, black and white, so he never got the colours of the symbol. But it was on the woman's shoulder. And she wasn't African but a coastal dweller off Jamaica. And a white woman, Scandinavian by the look of her.

The woman with the tattoo swam towards his end of the pool before resting up at the edge, arms sitting on the lip of the pool letting the water splash up against them. Only a few feet away, Austerley tried to study the tattoo beneath the water but such was the commotion of the liquid, he couldn't make anything out. Although right beside him, the woman ignored Austerley, instead, scanning around the pool. And like a hawk spotting its prey, her eyes suddenly honed in on a subject, and Austerley watched her begin to tense. Kirkgordon would be disgusted with this obvious show, as the woman seemed to be making no effort to conceal her watching of the target.

Tracing her stare, Austerley nearly choked when he saw the prey. Having shed the delightful rags she had been wearing at the dockside, the woman who had spoken to Kirkgordon, Dr Howard's associate, was now in a bikini, preparing to enter the pool. Looking around quickly, Austerley saw she was alone and seemingly oblivious of being watched. As she entered the pool, the African woman left the side of the pool and began to swim towards her target.

Austerley was unsure of what to do. *This is a fight, I don't do stand-up fighting. Where's Churchy? I need Churchy for this.* Like a sleek fish beneath the water, the African woman glided. Austerley thought he could see a knife beneath the water. Glancing up, Dr Howard's associate seemed unaware except that her hands were making some strange shapes. It was subtle, barely perceptible, but Austerley saw the formation and knew what was coming. Throwing his straw hat to the wind, he jumped into the pool causing some sun worshippers behind him to take a soaking.

The pool was only five feet deep, and Austerley, never the greatest swimmer, was thankful as he tried to work his way across the pool. The air was alive with magic, he could taste it, black and putrid. There was an evil taint to it. But there was also something in the water. Invisible but moving, he could see the water displacement of something long and thin. He struggled to keep a pace and watched in horror as the shape reached the African woman. It grabbed her neck encircling itself tight like a snake. And she began to thrash.

Chanting beneath his breath, Austerley made a shape with his hands and fought hard to endure the growing energy his body was taking on. He'd need to hold it a few moments longer if it was to be effective. Letting go, the floor of the pool saw a flame streak out and reach the invisible creature around the African woman's neck. There was a sudden and intense series of bubbles which formed around the woman's neck and rose quickly to the surface, causing it to foam slightly.

Desperately pushing forward in the water, Austerley reached the woman and lifted her to the surface. As she broke the water into the air, she coughed and spluttered violently and Austerley felt her weight being transferred from the water to him and he crashed back in, taking his casualty with him. His neck was grabbed a few seconds later and a voice was telling him it was alright. Assisted to the side of the pool, he saw the African woman being laid at the poolside, alive but obviously still recovering from her ordeal. A glance to where the perpetrator had been, saw him receive a dark stare of wild eyes from Dr Howard's associate.

"We appreciate the effort, sir, but you should really leave the saving lives up to our lifeguards. They are trained for this sort of thing, you could have compromised yourself," said a voice beside Austerley.

"I think I already have," Austerley replied and waved away further assistance. "Is she okay?"

"She is fine," said the woman.

"Good. We should really get you back to your cabin, let you have a rest."

"The ship's doctor will be here soon, he can examine her, make sure she's alright."

"That's appreciated," said Austerley, grabbing the lifeguard's hand and shaking it furiously, "but it's all fine. Reach me a towel and I'll make sure she's alright."

Austerley leaned close to the woman. "What are you doing? Are you wanting some sort of favour for your actions? That will not end well."

"Shut up," whispered Austerley, "I think that thing bit you and I may be the only person on this boat who can deal with a supernatural poison. So shut it, follow me and live."

The woman's eyes bulged in horror but she got to her feet and grabbed a towel. Together they walked towards the nearest set of lifts, watched closely by the associate of Dr Howard.

"James," said the lifeguard to his colleague, "do you smell cooked meat?"

"Yes, I do. But the grill's at the other pool. And that smell. It's like snake."

"Snake?"

23

"Yes, I had it on a safari. You don't forget that smell."

*****

Samantha was still on Kirkgordon's mind as he made his way back to the suite, ready to plan a recce on Dr Howard's suite that night. From the plans, it wasn't easy to sneak around the suite due to the open access and other people who might be wandering to their own cabins. Also, there was only one door to the suite so getting in, especially past the big guy he had met, might not be that easy. He would probably need to approach from outside. That would need planning.

Swiping the room card at the door of his suite, Kirkgordon pushed open the door and immediately tensed. There was a woman's scent in the air but he doubted Austerley had wooed one to his room. Letting the door close behind him, he went down on a knee behind a nearby chair. He heard the bed in Austerley's room tweak, like someone was on it and then got up and scanned the interior cabin. Soundlessly gliding across the living area, he checked the balcony was clear. Then passing the bathroom, he knocked open the door quietly and saw no one inside. After searching his own room, he came back to Austerley's bedroom and waited outside the door.

"I will break you, little man, if you do not hurry."

"These things take time. Just be patient and I'll sort you out."

Kirkgordon knew the bluff in Austerley's voice. His arm opened up and the small crossbow and bolt appeared. Turning into the room, Kirkgordon was surprised to find an African woman in just a bikini and towel. But she tensed into a fighting position when she saw him and Kirkgordon aimed the bolt straight at her.

"Who the hell's this? Are there any more? And why are you

bluffing?"

"Bluffing?" said the woman. "You are lying to me, little man. You said I was poisoned."

Kirkgordon laughed. "You're not the smoothest operator."

"It's not like that. She was attacked by the woman with Dr Howard. In the middle of her assassination attempt."

Kirkgordon took on a more heightened state of alertness. "She's an assassin? Turn over if you don't mind. Austerley get some rope."

"That sounds so dodgy…"

"Austerley, do it! If she's an assassin, we need to keep her hands contained. And why is she here for you?"

"Me," asked Austerley, "What makes you think she came for me?"

"I don't know, what could? I'm just surprised I haven't sent her myself."

Austerley, having found some rope, moved cautiously towards the woman. Like a flash, she took the rope out of his hands and wrapped it around his throat as a bolt from Kirkgordon glanced her shoulder. Throwing Austerley into Kirkgordon, she raced out of the bedroom door. Pushing Austerley out of the way, Kirkgordon raced into the suite living area and saw the woman's feet disappearing off the balcony. As he reached the edge and looked down to the sea, he saw her form diving into the water.

5

The Librarian

"What the hell is going on here?" raged Kirkgordon, reaching for a bottle of water from the mini-bar. "Vampires, assassins, some mad Doctor doing something that we don't know yet…I was going to have a relaxing time of it."

"Since when did they ever send us somewhere safe?" grumped Austerley. "She had a symbol on her leg. I've seen it before, long time ago. Not sure what it means."

"What symbol?"

"Trident, raised by a hand, seaweed wrapped around. It's in my head somewhere, but I can't get it out. I'm going to the library."

"The ship's library? I thought you said you wouldn't get anything there."

"You'd think not, but Wilson said different."

"When?" Kirkgordon shot back. "When was this great piece of advice?"

"When he briefed me. Separate from our main briefings. He was telling me about the possible legends of the area and the like. Waste of time really, as I know more about them than he does. But he did say he'd slip a few books into the library for me. General stuff. Well…not that general. But that symbol's got something to do with the sea."

Kirkgordon shook his head. "A trident. Seaweed. Hand rising up. It's got something to do with the sea. Even I got that bit."

"No. This sea. Can't remember what. Anyway, I'm going to the library. What are you going to do?"

"Plan. I need to get into the good Doctor's room and see what's happening. Hopefully he likes some entertainment. I'll do it tonight, early morning. Won't need you."

"Damn right you won't but speak to me before you go. I'll need to sort you some protection."

Kirkgordon stared incredulously at Austerley. "What protection?"

"Just some basic stuff. Charms and spells. Magic. All the stuff you don't know about."

"Piss off and read. Don't get into any trouble. Have you got your alerter?"

"No!"

"Damn well take it. You got yourself in enough bother with that assassin."

Austerley grabbed a glass of water and downed its contents. "She was co-operative and happy until you showed up. And I saved her life."

"Just take the damned alerter."

Austerley reluctantly reached into a top drawer of the desk and took a small device. Pocketing it, he turned away and shuffled out the door, leaving Kirkgordon to his plans.

There was too much commotion on the main promenade

and Austerley found himself feeling very claustrophobic until he arrived at the library. Once inside he was greeted by a young woman in a smart ship's uniform with her hair tied back and a name badge that read "Hannah."

"Ah, Professor. I assume you are here for your package from the university."

Austerley was taken aback. Miskatonic knew he was here? He hadn't worked for them since the graveyard incident, how did they know he was here? Strange.

"No, I'm here for the package from SET…"

"I think not, Professor," interrupted the woman quickly. "That particular acronym means something else here. I believe you are looking for your papers from the university."

"No I am not! I am looking for…"

"Your university papers, sent to you by Professor Wilson! Your good friend, Professor Wilson. And if you need help I am an expert in the languages of this area."

"It's fine, I happen to know a few languages myself," smirked Austerley, glad to put this young upstart in her place. The people they gave jobs to, it was ridiculous.

"Yes but some of these are strange, with peculiar local dialects I can help with, Professor."

"No, it's fine."

A piece of paper was shoved under Austerley's nose. The woman spoke under her breath.

"Tell me you can damn well read that, Einstein. Now shut your trap and go into one of the private reading rooms where I will join you. Wilson said you were an arse."

The woman had spoken in an East Coast accent, possibly Maine. But with the arse comment, the accent had also fallen. English. The bloody English. Little trumped up know-it-all.

Didn't she know she was talking to a Scotsman?

Austerley entered a booth at the rear of the library, followed by the woman holding a number of files and books. She laid them carefully on a large table behind which Austerley had positioned himself. Grabbing a large volume he opened it, and immediately swore.

"Why has he sent me this? This isn't the original language, in fact what language is this? It was only published in the original. Klaepikado tried to do an English translation but that clown couldn't translate a menu, so who's done this? Woman, what is this nonsense?"

The woman raised her eyes and drew her breath in hard through her nostrils, and Austerley thought he was a child at school who had spoken out of turn.

"Do you seriously think Professor Wilson would have sent a book like that in a language anyone could understand? It's encoded. Deeply encoded. One even you couldn't break from scratch. Unlike yourself, the Professor is a bit more cautious with the dangerous things of the world."

The woman came around behind Austerley and leaned over his shoulder, being extremely careful, so Austerley reckoned, to not touch him in any way. A whiff of delicate perfume struck his nose which whilst not unpleasant, didn't endear the woman to himself.

"My name is Hannah. Not, woman. Call me woman again and I'll walk out of here. Now, what would you like translated, sir. Simply open a page and I'll translate for you."

"Just give me the code and I'll work alone."

"It's four version deep, rotating around whatever two characters come in front of it. You'd need at least half a book's worth to crack it if you had the translation so just tell me what you need and I'll translate."

Austerley was impressed. "And you are holding that in your head? That's not bad. Do you have a photographic memory?"

The woman shook her head and whispered in Austerley's ear. "No, and there's nothing freakish about me, just a damn good learner and a hard worker. Not your sort of woman, I hear."

Puzzled by this attack on his person, Austerley regrouped by opening the volume to what he thought was the page he wanted. There was a drawing in the top right hand corner which showed a trident and a hand with some discolouration around it. "There. Read there. From the top to the bottom of the page."

The woman looked at him apparently awaiting something. "Please."

Austerley listened intently as the woman spoke without hesitation, detailing a history of discovery of the symbol. Believed to have been from ancient times, its first recording in writing was from the ancient Greeks, a sea captain recording it on a stowaway. Then there was a symbol found in a cave on the coast of Jamaica. America had a few sightings on strangers in various cities. Most recently it had been seen within the last one hundred years on travellers on trading ships moving around or near the Bermuda Triangle. A total of maybe fifteen sightings throughout history.

"That was impressive," said Austerley, "Where did you study?"

"Oxford until the service took me out. My cousin has connections. He did call you an arse also."

"People are so damn pass remarkable!"

"No, he's not. He was warning me in case I ever met you."

"It's Havers, isn't it? Your cousin is Havers. There's something in your detachment from things. The way you leant over my shoulder. Cautious but still getting the job done. Abrupt to the point of moving things on."

"Very good, Mr Austerley. What happened to him? Wilson never said. Confidential. It would take a lot to kill my cousin, what happened to him? You were on the mission beyond. The mission to…" She said a word which Austerley recognised, the correct word for the Nether Lands they had visited trying to rescue Kirkgordon's wife. A language very few knew. Not even Havers. And here she was reciting the word perfectly. There was more to this woman than he had thought.

"He was intent on getting to Farthington, your cousin kind of went nuts after his friend the priest died at Farthington's hands. Or breath actually."

"The priest was a former partner in the agency. They had their differences but they were once brothers in arms and very close. Not many get close to my cousin."

"Well, we were on a platform suspended above an opening to Dagon's realm, and I believe your cousin took Farthington off it and dropped them both to their doom. I didn't actually see it as I was hanging on a rope at the time. He wasn't right after the death of the holy man. He wanted to cut my foot off."

"Surprised it wasn't your head." The woman seemed to be far off thinking about something. She was lithe like Havers, elegant, but also with a face which was attractive enough, but also easily forgettable.

"I think I can manage from here," said Austerley.

"But you've only had a page read."

"The code's not that difficult. Are they all the same code? I mean all the papers and volumes." He saw the woman shake her head. "If I need another volume, I'll rap the window."

The woman stepped away towards the door, evidently still in a morose thought about her cousin.

"That pronunciation of the Nether Lands. Very impressive. I've never heard anyone say it that well, at least not on this side of the portal. Your cousin didn't even know the name."

"Well, no, Arthur may have his understanding of things but really at heart he's a man of action. *Was* a man of action. I was the bookworm of the family."

"When we're back at base, if you are ever at base, and you want a few lessons, let me know. Don't waste your mind."

The woman tutted. "I hardly think I've wasted my mind. And unlike you, mine is still intact."

The door shut and Austerley was left alone. *Yes, incredibly good pronunciation*.

6

A Little Night Excursion

Thankfully the night had become somewhat cloudy, making this excursion somewhat easier than it might have been. As he pulled on the last glove, Kirkgordon checked his outfit in the mirror. The balaclava covered his whole face except for a couple of eye slits, leaving this as the only exposed area in an otherwise perfect sea of black. Even his arm was wrapped tight although the costume could accommodate the opening of his weaponry contained within the forearm.

Thankfully, Austerley hadn't come back, allowing Kirkgordon a little rest and solitude to plan this reconnaissance. Sometimes he just got in the way with all his mumbo jumbo talk. Obviously the books Wilson had sent along had been up to scratch or maybe he was just stuffing his face. Austerley always seemed capable of eating, possibly the cause of his vast size, although he was more of a hulk than a fatty.

Turning off his cabin lights, Kirkgordon allowed his eyes to adjust to the dark before stepping outside to the balcony of the berth. The midnight buffet would now be in full swing, so those who hadn't gone to their beds would be engaged in feeding, gambling or one of the other many interior distractions the vessel afforded. Kirkgordon doubted there would be many out looking down at the side of the boat. They were in the middle of the sea now with no land to look at. No, the films under the stars would be keeping watchful eyes away.

Taking the sucker pads onto his hands, he flung himself above his balcony, threading along the thin line of metal between the two decks which separated the balconies of the different cabins. Quickly, he made his way to the end of a row of balconies and onto a larger expanse of metal where he paused momentarily to get his bearings. Dr Howard's suite occupied the front end of the vessel, three decks from the very top of the ship.

With an alacrity defying his age, Kirkgordon quickly worked his way to the underside of the smallest balcony associated with Dr Howard's suite. That would be the private view of his associate most probably. He knew the layout of the suite and the smallest balcony led to the minor bedroom, so maybe a bodyguard or associate. He would have to wait and see if this preferred route was available, but if not he had other ideas involving distraction. Ideally, he wanted to be in and out without any commotion or suspicion.

Hanging underneath the small balcony, Kirkgordon listened intently but heard no obvious noise other than the crashing waves below and the sound of the movie showing a deck or so above. Gingerly, he raised himself until he could see through the plastic protective wall of the balcony. Everything was dark. A small white table and chair on the balcony sat alone, barren. Staring intently, he tried to see the interior of the cabin but the light was too poor. *Nothing for it.* Quickly, but silently,

Kirkgordon clambered over the protective wall and set down onto the balcony floor.

Edging along the side wall, he checked the cabin and saw some low units with various jewellery and clothing atop. More clothing covered what appeared to be a chair. The clothing was for a large man, and Kirkgordon found the owner when his attention turned to the bed. Closest to him were the bare buttocks of a well-toned man, maybe six foot or more. The bed's covers lay partially over his legs and there was a pillow on the floor.

Beyond the man was the figure of a woman, but Kirkgordon found it hard to see much more detail other than a curve covered by a single sheet, curves that could only be female. Kirkgordon stood for a full minute waiting to observe the state of the sleepers. Watching for the rhythmic breathing that denoted a true sleeper, he was relieved to see that they were showing no signs of tension or apprehension that someone in wait would display.

The door into the cabin was a sliding patio style contraption that moved back soundlessly and he slipped inside, eyes on the sleeping pair. Quickly, he opened the drawers of the furniture in the room but found them mainly empty except for clothing and the odd trinket. As he edged past the sleepers, the man rolled slightly causing the covers to fall off completely, including from the woman. Kirkgordon slunk into the corner of the room and knelt down. He saw the woman rise up and grab the covers back over her body. Her figure was dazzling and he recognised her as the woman from the car, the woman Austerley had seen being targeted, who had sent her assassin such an unwelcome present.

It was five minutes before Kirkgordon resumed, and he

decided to move into the larger area beyond this bedroom. The door was locked from the inside, and he delicately turned the mechanism. On opening, he saw the camera just above the door pointing out into the room. Carefully he climbed the wall with his suckers until he was behind the camera. Removing his mobile, he took a picture of the room, as close to the camera as he could. Spinning the screen around, he held it in front of the camera. A quick dose of tape held it in position. Thankfully the camera wasn't that advanced and he doubted it would be screening for infrared or night vision.

The suite was large and he remembered from the plans that the bathroom was at the far corner along with a sitting room. There was a spiral staircase leading to a floor above which would have the master bedroom and a small office. Looking around, Kirkgordon decided as he had previously thought, that the office would be where most of the best material would be stored.

There was a sudden flicker of motion from the outside balcony of the main living area and the patio door slid open. Thankfully the lights didn't switch on as a large figure made its way to the small kitchenette. Kirkgordon had slid behind a curtain and remained there as he heard a kettle boil before the figure returned to the balcony, carrying a delicate china cup of some steaming liquid. Kirkgordon was unperturbed by this interruption and glided onto the spiral staircase and deftly climbed to the upper floor. Standing beside the bedroom door, he listened for the breathing of its occupant. There was nothing. Maybe he was out.

With soundless steps, he entered the office area and sought out something of use. There was a filing cabinet, obviously part of the furniture. A large desk was covered in sailing magazines and pictures of islands. The room was dark, but Kirkgordon was loathe to turn on a light or use his torch. A small briefcase was on the desk, and Kirkgordon decided this was the real lock up in the room.

There were two clasps on the front of the case and Kirkgordon got close to study them further. He recognised the brand and the trap mechanism. Turning the case over, he checked the rim of the item. With gentle hands he traced the lines and contours until he felt the slight imperfection. With a delicate press, a panel in the bottom end opened and revealed a space capable of holding maybe twenty sheets of A4. Gingerly, Kirkgordon took out the paper within. Using a small scanner, he quickly took pictures of the paper without using any light. He only looked briefly at the words on the sheets but he understood none of them. Still, it should keep Austerley busy.

There was a light on downstairs and Kirkgordon heard footsteps coming up the stairs. He doubted he would have time to make an exit from the room and quickly sealed the briefcase back up, placing it back in its original position, before curling up in the well of the desk, hidden from the door. Feet entered the office and he heard the briefcase being picked up. The shoes were leather, smart and brown, and accompanied some tailored trousers. It was probably the Doctor.

The lights went off and Kirkgordon held his position for ten minutes, during which he heard some mutterings between Dr Howard and his guard. There was a request to check the cargo, deck five, compartment ten bravo. And then darkness and silence.

Satisfied that the suite had settled back to its previous quiet, Kirkgordon edged out to the upper landing. Carefully scanning below, he descended the spiral staircase and reached up to the mobile he had positioned. He heard a commotion in the small room and the sound of someone coming towards the door in a rough fashion. Instinctively, he quickly scampered up the wall and hung on the ceiling over the door. He could see the guard on the large balcony stir and begin to come to the patio door. He was in the darkest corner of the suite but if the lights went on, they would see him straight away. He allowed his crossbow to emerge from his forearm, bolt loaded.

Beneath him, the door flung open with the room's occupants gripped together in a naked embrace. Passions were being laid out for anyone to see. The sweating figures passed below Kirkgordon with grunts and groans, deep murmurs of delight. Eyes focused on the frisky couple lest they spot him, Kirkgordon also sneaked quick glances towards the guard. He seemed to be laughing and then returned to his seat on the balcony.

Taking the moment, Kirkgordon fell silently to the floor and opened the door before shutting it quickly behind him. Knowing the couple could return any second, he tore across the bedroom and hurriedly opened the patio door. Keen to not leave any trace of his excursion, he closed the door and then quickly descended a few decks on the vessel's outside. Only then did he breathe easy, deep, long breaths that sought to let out the tension he had felt.

There had to be something in the cargo bay worth seeing. He had some paperwork but it would take Austerley to know if it was of any use. If it wasn't there, it would be a wasted trip, and he'd check the cargo anyway. But the guard was on the move to it. It could disappear, or worse, be used. No, he needed to check the cargo out now.

Deck 5 and compartment ten bravo. Well, he could get to deck 5 easy enough, but as for where ten bravo was, he'd need to search. Still, it was early enough. Looking down the ship, he tried to work out just where he could get access to deck 5 as it was far below. There was the launch access for the little boats that took travellers ashore but that would be shut up. No, he'd have to go in a few decks up and probably shed the *darks* he was wearing.

As Kirkgordon began to move off he was aware of something watching him. Something close. And then it dawned on him there was a woman beside him. Pale in complexion, in an evening dress and hanging onto the side with no suction cups or other apparatus, the woman smiled. Her lips were shabby and drained but it was the white teeth that protruded at either corner that bothered Kirkgordon.

"Where is Mr Austerley? I do hope he doesn't mind me having a bite."

7

Uninvited Guest

Kirkgordon froze. He'd never seen a vampire like this. The one in the vessel's hallway that Austerley fell over had more colour on her lips than this one. The moment was surreal, his eyes taken to a figure hugging dress that screamed out all the creature's feminine attributes, while the hunger in the eyes seemed passionate until you took in the fangs protruding from the mouth. Alana said that some men looked at her as if she was just meat. Kirkgordon had never fully understood that feeling…until now.

"You might not want to do that." It was the only thing that came into Kirkgordon's head and he noted the cliché. Surely heroes had better one liners than this.

The vampire, with dark, silky hair, merely inched closer, placing her face right in front of Kirkgordon's. "Someone's feisty."

"You might not realise, but I am armed."

"Oh, more fun. I don't think you have the kind of weapons needed for me. It has been a long time since my last male. Maybe I'll love you before I leave you."

A shiver ran through Kirkgordon and he found himself staring deep into the creature's eyes. Something in the back of his head told him that was how they entrapped their prey, but the front was doing all the thinking. His eyes only flickered from the creature's eyes to its body and then back, drinking in the view. And yet, it was an entrancement, rather than a hunger. He couldn't pull away even though his fate was obvious to his mind.

The vampire leaned forward and Kirkgordon tried to adjust his position for a better focus. But with his mind on the creature, his poise in finding the ship's hull with his sucker pads was impaired and he tumbled off the side.

The arm opened up and a bolt with a rope attached fired off, piercing the side of the hull. Kirkgordon swung hard into the vessel's side and was left hanging by his arm. The pain made him react quickly, reaching up with his other hand and he began to swing, looking for a balcony to land on. Unsure how far he had fallen he was oblivious to what deck he was on but he could see a line of small balconies to his left. Above him he heard nails scratching on metal. Without looking up, he concentrated on where he would land and let go just in front of a balcony.

Clipping his feet on its rail, Kirkgordon flipped, landing eventually on his shoulders with a crash. There was movement inside the balcony's cabin and Kirkgordon forced himself to leap up and grab the lip of the balcony. Hauling himself to the front, he saw the cabin's light come on so he held himself on the hull's side between the balcony above and that below.

Someone stepped out on the balcony below but Kirkgordon was scanning the area for the vampire. He didn't want to involve the cabin's occupants and have a death on his hands, but he also needed to get away, or to keep safe somehow.

"Shush, don't make a noise, and he'll not see us."

Closing his eyes, Kirkgordon listened for anything betraying the vampire's movements. The person on the balcony was damn noisy as they seemingly checked the area. That, coupled with the gentle breaking of waves below, meant he had difficulty picking anything out. But there was just a breath. And she was moving closer. Kirkgordon could hear another cabin occupant and a voice he recognised.

That's Sam's voice. But not the same balcony, slightly further away, next to it maybe. That's a route in. I can take that route in.

The man below had seemingly given up on his search and sounded something off in a foreign language. Kirkgordon opened his eyes and realised that the balcony below had gone dark but the one beside was lit. *Hell, Sam, no. Get inside.*

Kirkgordon thought *rope* and then fired the bolt into the ship's hull. Letting go, he allowed himself to fall until he was in line with the lighted balcony. He had to lash out a foot to push, and then swing, towards the open gap before letting the rope go.

Sam was standing aghast in just a short dressing gown, her bare legs showing from the mid-thigh down. As Kirkgordon recovered from his landing, he saw the shock on her face but her eyes were looking behind him. And that glazed look he had so recently held was evident.

Kirkgordon grabbed Sam by the shoulders and planted a deep kiss on her lips. When she didn't respond, he drove deeper with the kiss until he felt her mouth respond. Without hesitation, he grabbed her legs from under her and carried her quickly towards the open door behind her leading to her cabin. Stepping over the threshold, he heard a voice behind

42

him.

"Two, such a feast to have two. And she's so delicious a body too. But it's really your blood I want." The creature, still resplendent in its evening wear strode towards the door.

"Back or I'll take you apart," warned Kirkgordon.

"Hardly. You were lucky to fall from my grasp before. Come, let me taste that red wine of yours. A spirited man like you will be a delight to the palate."

"I'll burn you. You've seen my arm. I'll set you ablaze." Kirkgordon felt his arm being grabbed hard and could hear Sam's heavy breathing, her body shaking.

"I think I'll take my chances."

Kirkgordon was starting to panic. He wasn't sure he could keep the creature back. Would the fire bolt be enough? Why wasn't there a wooden stake option? And with Sam in his arms, his fighting skills were severely hampered. This was going to the wire. He caught the vampire's glare. He felt the hypnotic eyes burn into him. Belonging. Ownership. Mistress.

"You're not welcome. This is my cabin and you are not invited in. He is, but you're not. Stay out. And while you're at it, get off my bloody balcony."

With an unholy curse the vampire suddenly exploded into a fog that drifted off to the night. Kirkgordon stood and stared at the night, holding a now weeping Sam to his chest. *That was too close. This was meant to be an easy run, surveillance job, and bit of relaxation. But now, vampires. And not even my target.*

"What the hell was that?" mumbled Sam.

"A vampire," answered Kirkgordon.

"Of course it was a bloody vampire. That's why I told it that it wasn't welcome in. I mean you with a rope in your arm, landing here, and also the bloody vampire. What the hell? Just who are you. And bloody kissing me like that too."

"Ah well, I needed to kiss you, because of the vampire stare. Break the link."

"Well that's gotta be one of the lamest… And what about the rest of it. Are you a robot?"

"No, no I'm not. My arm is a special appendage I had made when I lost my arm and hand to cold."

"Most people get a simple prosthetic. Why does yours have a rope?"

"Easy! I just saved your damn life."

There was no response. Sam simply erupted into a wild sobbing, and her body shook. Kirkgordon held her close, tightly to absorb the shaking. He had forgotten how these things made people react. When he worked with the team, they had all been experienced in the strange, the weird and downright evil. Sam had just been hit with a reality check that was being cashed in big time.

After a short while, she stopped sobbing, and Kirkgordon let her legs down but held onto her shoulders, looking into her eyes for comprehension. "You okay?" Her dressing gown was soaked with sweat and she cut a sweet figure, but her distress was taking away any enjoyable thoughts he might have had.

"You were up for fun. That seems a bit too much. Who are you?"

Kirkgordon wondered how much to tell her and if she could handle it. He was strictly undercover but just how well that was working was another matter. Austerley's bloody loud shirts. Still, making alliances was part of the game wasn't it?

"I'm government." *Damn, that's the bit I shouldn't mention.*

"Whose?"

"What? Ours!"

"I'm guessing it's not Revenue and Customs. MI6?"

"No. SETAA."

"Who? Never heard of them."

"Well you won't have. We're very secret. Only Her Majesty really knows."

"Now you're making this up. You expect me to believe the Queen's running a secret operation no one else knows about."

"No. Obviously, some people know."

"Who? Who else knows?"

"I can't say. Said too much already. I need to go, Sam. Got things to do. I suggest you just go back to bed."

"Seriously? Just pop back to bed? I just had a vampire on my balcony."

"Which you forbade entry too. Which I didn't know you could do. Where did you learn that?"

Sam shook her head. "The movies. You didn't know that?"

Kirkgordon shook his head. "My first vampire. More used to men with frog and fish heads."

Sam stared hard at him, searching his eyes. "You're telling the truth, aren't you? Unbelievable. This shit is really true. It's really…" She started to shake again and Kirkgordon took her by the shoulders.

"Okay, you're in shock. You need a drink and a lie down. I'll fix you a whiskey and then get yourself to bed."

"You are not leaving me."

"I have to go."

"Then I'm coming. Or dammit, I'll tell the whole ship."

She will and all, looking at her now. Oh hell, at least Wilson isn't here to give me a talk from the boss about how to handle the public. Containment, that's what he'd say, keep it contained, don't let the talk get out.

"Okay, you can come with me. But we need to go now."

"After I shower. I need to clean up, I must stink by now with all this sweat. I look a mess."

"Actually you look…"

"What?"

"Just go shower. I'll wait here." She grimaced but then turned away to her bathroom in the small cabin. *Cos you look fantastic. You look so good. Dammit, Austerley's going to have a field day when he finds her in our cabin.*

With a sense of propriety that insisted to be heard rather than one which was embraced, Kirkgordon opened the balcony door and stood outside looking out to sea. A rope swung and gently caught him on his head. *Yeah I'd better get rid of the evidence of that encounter. And I'd better do it before she gets out of the shower.*

8

Baggage Search

"Sam, probably best if you put some black clothes on, or at least really dark stuff. No heels either. Tie your hair up. Actually no, leave it down for now but bring a hair tie. And no skirts or dresses, rather jeans or leggings or..."

Kirkgordon stopped his helpful advice when he saw Sam emerge from her bathroom with a floppy dark grey jumper on with black leggings and trainers. Looking nervous but more composed than she had done some ten minutes ago, she stood there awaiting approval.

"Yeah, good. Now listen, whatever happens get behind me if anyone comes at us. Hopefully we won't get any more surprises but you never know when you go snooping."

"We're going snooping? Why? I thought we'd be going somewhere safe. Somewhere protected."

Kirkgordon watched her face fall again and realised she needed picked up.

"We will. We definitely will, but right now I have to check something out. But you'll be with me. I will protect you, it's what I do." The woman nodded, but Kirkgordon wondered how much she believed him.

"We need to go down the decks, to the cargo holds, so I can see what's come on board. There shouldn't be trouble but… you never know." He took Sam's hand and led her to her cabin door. With a quick smile to her, he then opened the door and walked out into the rather tight corridor of a thousand doors. *Dammit, they pack them in down in the common class.*

"Keep hold of my hand. It'll look more natural, and I can guide you on where we are going. Try and breathe normally and don't *not* look at people. It's important to do what you normally would." He could feel her shaking as he told her the simple instructions and wondered if this really was a good idea. Still, she had thought quickly in the cabin.

They wandered the corridor until they reached the elevator, where Kirkgordon pressed the call button. Checking up and down the lit corridor, he kept giving brief smiles at Sam but she didn't respond. After a bright bing, the elevator opened its doors and they stepped into a well-appointed metallic elevator with a large mirror on one side. After pressing the button for the lowest floor he could find, Kirkgordon noticed Sam staring at him in the mirror.

"What?"

"At least you're not a vampire."

"Why?"

"The mirror. They don't show a reflection."

"You seem quite the expert." This caused Sam to smile, and Kirkgordon breathed a little easier. He needed her to unwind or she would be so obvious if anyone was watching.

The elevator stopped at deck seven, and the doors opened to another long corridor. They walked along it until Kirkgordon found a door marked "staff only". There was a swipe card access and Kirkgordon looked for any crew but there were none forthcoming.

"Keep an eye on the corridor while I work on this." Sam nodded and stepped back. Carefully Kirkgordon took a small scanning light from his clothing. It showed up fingerprints if shone in the dark but the corridor was too light and he was forced to cover it up with one hand. Carefully he looked in and saw four of the buttons had a mass of fingerprints on them. Four, seven, five and…

A hand grabbed his shoulder spinning him around. Sam's face was right there and she tilted her neck, driving her mouth towards his. He gave in to her forceful intrusion and then felt her hands reach inside his top, rubbing his back. She broke off the kiss momentarily to whisper, "Take a proper hold of me."

Holding back, he suddenly understood when the door behind him opened. He raced his hands up under her sweater and felt her pull him close snaking a leg around him. There was a tut behind him and someone walking away. And despite the strong distraction that Sam's ruse was affording, he slipped a leg backwards and stopped the door from closing by only a fraction of an inch. They continued to fumble until Kirkgordon snatched a glance at the corridor and saw the crew person had gone.

"Okay, enough," said Kirkgordon. He could barely contain his disbelief when she looked affronted. "The door is open, just about, and we need to move however nice this is."

Sam nodded and released him. Turning, he opened the door and peered into an area that descended down in steps that seemed to form a staircase to the lower decks. He pulled

Sam through and together they slowly descended. At the next level they saw the words "Secondary Gallery", "Preparations Rooms", "Entertainment Services" and "Medical Centre". But it was the large "Deck Six" legend that Kirkgordon was most interested in. He motioned to Sam that they needed to go down further.

Again holding her hand they descended, and he became aware of how loud she was. Not that her feet were thudding everywhere, but to someone used to sneaking about, she sounded like an elephant. Still, it hardly mattered here. But maybe later it would.

Another door appeared and the legend "Deck Five" was emblazoned on it. He could see through a window a small deck map in the corridor. And he also heard someone approaching the door. *Up or down, what way would they be going? Middle of the night, surely down to quarters. So away from the door.*

Kirkgordon grabbed Sam and made her crouch down adjacent to where the door would open. Holding her tight, he watched the door open and then quickly clasped a hand over her mouth, stifling a gasp. As the door swung closed, they saw a man in uniform disappear down the staircase, oblivious of their presence. He held his hand across her mouth and whispered in her ear to stay low. Stepping around her, he listened to the corridor for a few seconds and then opened the door gently.

There were feet. More than one. And then laughing voices. A man and a woman. He let the door go and returned to his position behind Sam. He could feel her shaking and held her by the shoulders. His hand returned to her mouth, keeping it covered. The door opened again and the couple walked through it, engaged in some conversation about another worker who had apparently put on some weight.

Bitchy or what? Time to move.

Kirkgordon waited until the couple had let go of the door and then grabbed the handle. As the complaining pair walked away he spun around the door dragging Sam through before pulling the door significantly closer to its frame. Then he let it go. It sounded shut in about the same time as it normally would.

He glanced at the deck plan on the wall and realised that the small cargo area on this deck was to the forward and immediately pulled Sam off along what was a drab corridor with pipes and valves. Quickly, the wall became little holds, shelving with numbers above it. Delta Three. Delta Four. Delta…

A voice. Looking left, Kirkgordon saw Delta Four had a drop cover which he pulled up revealing a few cases. There was a gap above them and he turned and swept Sam off her feet, letting her roll over the cases and drop into the void behind. He then threw himself in, pausing to pull down the cover behind him. With a flick of his hips, he rolled off the cases and fell on top of Sam.

He heard her small cry of pain as he landed on her and then realised her head was above his. He raised a hand and covered her mouth. He tried not to think about the position he was in, not the danger from the people in the corridor but rather the compromising position his head was in. He heard her heart beat, and her quick breathing was being relayed in intimate detail. *Austerley would have a field day!*

He heard voices coming closer and lay perfectly still. Having done this many times before, Kirkgordon was at ease with the situation. There was no reason for anyone to check the compartments, he was in a reasonably safe place. And he was armed if it came to anything. But Sam wasn't so comfortable and was quivering with fear. *Poor girl. First vampires and now this. I did tell her to stay, though.*

The voices stopped momentarily in front of their compartment and Kirkgordon silenced a wince as Sam's nails dug into him. Their language sounded South American but in reality, Kirkgordon didn't know. It was hard to admit, but sometimes not having Austerley left him exposed on a lot of fronts. Like with the vampire, Austerley would have known what Sam knew and a whole lot more.

Waiting a full two minutes after the voices had moved on, Kirkgordon climbed out from the compartment and then helped his companion back to the corridor.

"Sorry for the closeness."

"No," murmured Sam, "close was good. They were so near." He saw her still trembling. They needed to move, get going, get air through her body, and calm her nerves. *Where's ten bravo?*

Taking her hand, Kirkgordon tried not to think about lying close to Sam in the compartment and how her scent kept pervading his protective thoughts, distracting him from his watch. He knew women were his downfall. First Alana had been the woman who could keep him in check but then Calandra had shown up when his marriage had gotten rough. With her staying away, Sam had moved in as a bit of company for this trip, but as usual, he was struggling to keep her there in his thoughts. It wasn't easy being a man.

On the good side of wandering the ship at this late hour—or was it early?—there were very few crew about, especially here in the cargo deck. Tracing his way from another plan on the wall, Kirkgordon led Sam along some narrow corridors to more secure compartments. These had solid hatch covers and were locked with padlocks. The legends above each compartment soon showed the way to ten bravo.

Standing in front of the padlock, Kirkgordon removed some small tools from his clothing and worked quickly on the lock springing it easily. The door shot up and Sam let out a quick yell. There was a hiss from inside and on rising gently to the level of the compartment, Kirkgordon saw a snake's head inside. It was currently looking away from him, and he scanned the contents of the compartment, seeing only a few empty packets. Deftly, he placed his artificial hand inside and grabbed the packets. He felt Sam grip him tight as the snake turned its head.

There was a moment of standoff, brief but tense, as reptile looked at man. And then the creature dove its fangs into Kirkgordon's hand. Sam screamed and reached into the compartment grabbing the body of the snake but its fangs remained embedded in Kirkgordon's hand. But there was no pain. Only a sensation that said something was on his hand. *Artificial hands. At least they're good for something.*

"Flame," whispered Kirkgordon, and his arm opened and a bolt complete with flaming head appeared. Rolling his wrist he managed to make the yellow, dancing flame connect with the snake's body and the fangs released almost instantly. He barked a whisper at Sam to get clear. With his other arm, he slammed the door shut and then watched his arm weapon disappear back inside his appendage.

"What was that?"

"I don't really know but it got my artificial arm, so no harm done." He saw Sam still staring at the compartment. "No harm done. We need to go back to my cabin and regroup. I need my friend to look at these bags I collected. He'll know what to do with them."

"Your friend? Are you close?"

"Did I say friend? Should have said colleague."

And they were off quickly, moving back along the path they had come. But all was clear, and they managed to get back to the elevator on the main deck without incident. Kirkgordon laid back on the wall of the elevator and saw Sam staring at him. There was a breathlessness to her, still reeling from the excitement, but he saw something else too. He knew that look and fought the conceited feelings he was having about it. Stepping up to him, Sam turned around and laid into him, taking his arms and placing them around her. *Okay, just for now, I'm too dog-tired to fight it.* But he knew that wasn't true.

With a ding the elevator stopped at deck ten and before the caller could enter the elevator, Sam had turned around and was cuddling into Kirkgordon and planting a kiss on him.

"I think this is the way to stay undercover," she whispered. Although he thought she was technically right, Kirkgordon knew this was no cover. But there were worse ways to stay hidden. With half an eye, he saw two people enter the lift in perfect evening attire. The man was obviously of an age but he had incredibly good skin, if a little pale. The woman was a red head with a stunning green evening dress that flaunted all the right bits to attract a man. Again, she was just a little pale.

The doors closed and the lift began to move upwards when he felt Sam's grip tighten, but this was fear, not pleasure. She moved her head to one side and whispered in his ear.

"There's no reflection, oh God, there's nothing there."

9

Smooth Talking Austerley

T he crick that had been forming in his neck got too much for him, and Austerley reached out his arms and stretched. There really was so much packed into this volume, minute details that would be missed by many. And some of it an eye opener. Having done research into the area before, Austerley knew there was more to the Bermuda triangle legend than general knowledge or even significant knowledge, understood. But this volume gave some great detail and a great warning.

Having dealt with a number of forces that few people ever tap into, Austerley was slowly beginning to understand that tapping into any power made you a conduit and meant you started to take on the traits of the being or entity behind the power itself. Dagon still flowed through him and would frequent his dreams. But it also meant that anything related to Dagon happening in the locale would affect his sleep and mind. He would become the proverbial lightening rod.

Now he had never had experience of coming into contact with anything to do with the Bermuda Triangle, but the volume he had just read was advising that contact left a mark on you. Kirkgordon would no doubt see it as good or evil, a black and white notion, but really there were all sorts of powers coming from different angles of what was good or evil. After all, weren't the nations of the world like that?

Still, what time was it? Bloody hell! The clock in the room showed four a.m. Austerley stood up and began to collate the volume and rearrange it into its bindings. Nothing like a good read, but he was tired and needed some sleep. Carrying the papers to the door, he peered through the window and saw Hannah at the library welcome desk, apparently intently engaged in writing a letter. It appeared to be several pages long. She looked up as he opened the door.

"Did you get everything you need?" she asked, almost giving a smile.

"Yes. Thanks. Look, I get a little focused when doing these things, so if I was a bit obstreperous, then don't let it bother you."

"Most people say sorry, but my cousin said you don't tend to do that, Professor Austerley."

"Well, no. He's probably right on that… but then again he's not often wrong. Well… he wasn't often wrong before… well you know."

"No, Arthur rarely was."

Austerley glanced at the letter the woman was writing and saw it was in code. A code that seemed quite deep.

"You write in code?" he asked.

"Yes. I doubt you'd be able to break it. I designed it myself."

"Oh, I could. With maybe five or six words maximum."

"Four. You couldn't do it with four."

"Any four, name them?"

56

"There. That's *is*. And that's *sluice*. There, *but*. And that's *fridge*."

Austerley picked up the first sheet with Hannah watching him closely. For two minutes, his eyes raced over the letters and then he reached out with a free hand indicating he wanted the second page. After ten minutes and when Austerley was on his eighth page, Hannah stood up and tapped his shoulder.

"Okay, stop. What's it about? Go on, tell me."

"It's quite elegant in patches. Especially when you tell him to ram a hoover up his…"

"Okay! But who is he and what's it all about?"

Austerley looked up from the page and shook his head gently. "He seriously took on a married woman when he had you? And then tried to take the money? What an arse!"

"And?"

"Well, pages four to eight have a lot of legal jargon, but if you want my opinion, I'd cut and run because sub clause 4.5 of the divorce settlement has left you in a bit of a limbo. You can win it, but not without a lot of legal costs. So I'd cut him loose and just get on with life."

Austerley looked up and saw Hannah just staring at him, a little tearful. Sheepishly, Austerley handed back the pages.

"You weren't meant to crack it, Mr Austerley. Most people, having realised the sensitive nature of the discourse after page one would have just stopped. But then…"

"Ah, yes. I don't really do that relationship stuff well."

"Evidently. Do you require anything else?"

"No, no. I'm going to go back to the cabin, try and get some sleep. Try and focus on what I've learnt." Austerley forced a smile but the woman didn't seem to be warming back up to him.

"And what is it that you've learnt?"

"Well, it is here. A city under the water. At least one that was lost. And it's tied into deep running power. But I need to get back and talk to Kirkgordon. He's running the operation. He needs to know, get him off my back about the other things he doesn't know."

"Goodnight, Professor Austerley." Hannah was staring at him, practically throwing him out.

"Yes, goodnight. But just for the record, definitely better off without him. You could do a lot better." She looked back at Austerley staring and he felt somewhat uncomfortable, like he had been found lurking at the door of the women's showers. *But I am right.*

The main concourse had only a couple of people at the various bars, most of which seemed closed. Ship life didn't seem to extend to these small hours and was mainly relegated to a few cleaning crew scrubbing down the closed venues. After catching an elevator, Austerley made his way along a corridor before turning into the other end of the hallway from which his cabin was situated. As he went to stride forward and to his bed, he saw a fog drift around the corner far ahead.

Without hesitation, Austerley reached inside his pockets and took in his hands the small crucifix inside. It was always best to take care with vampires, as you never knew when they would hypnotise you and then drink you dry. *Hideous creatures.*

The fog came right up to Austerley, and he raised the crucifix before him. It was then that he felt the nip on the back of his hand and he dropped it. A rasping voice spoke from behind.

"Although yours would be a most delicious neck to feast on, I fear others want you for more sublime reasons. Still, never say never."

The hallway reeked of vampire. He hated the smell and taste of them but it seemed they were into warning their victims. He felt the nails on his throat.

"Our daughter has been adventuring tonight, and we apologise for her actions. I fear that she may have injured your friend and many others."

"Then you really should take greater care." It was Hannah. "Unhand Professor Austerley and then find your daughter, making sure she doesn't harm another soul on this ship. I presume there are coffins and soil on this vessel. Live there and stay there, otherwise I shall hunt you down."

Austerley was watching to see if the fight would happen but then saw the vampires change form again and slope away. Turning around he saw Hannah, complete with stake, in a braced positioned as if something was about to attack.

"Ah, you followed me."

"As Mr Kirkgordon sees fit not to look after the most dangerous man on the ship, then it falls on me to take charge."

"Well it's nice of you to say so."

"I meant dangerous like volatile. Liable to go off half-cocked and then come running back to mummy."

Austerley railed. "Now look here. There are some of us who need to uphold this world and protect it. If you had this kind of power and responsibility running through you then you might have the odd moment!"

"Exactly but when I go gaga I don't tend to total the world. Now if you don't mind, Professor, we should really go and find out if your colleague is okay."

"No we shouldn't," raged Austerley. "I have a bed to get to. You go get him and leave the ticking bomb alone." With that Austerley stormed off towards his cabin. Approaching it, he grabbed his key card and slid it into the slot allowing the door to open. Turning, he addressed Hannah, "So still with me then. Well, there's a mini bar and probably tea available for the pot, although who knows what the quality is like. If you're going to be here, then you might as well be useful."

Inside, he switched on the lights and made for his bedroom. Hearing Hannah put the kettle on, he combed his hair and then changed his shirt for a green Hawaiian with some particularly large palm trees as its centrepiece. On exiting the bedroom, he found Hannah waiting for him.

"Did Arthur say anything when he left the platform? Anything at all?"

"Not that I heard. He was obsessed. Farthington was everything to him, the only thing that mattered, while the fate of the world, no worlds, was at stake. Why do you ask?"

"It's just that I heard a few rumours. Nothing about him, just incidents around the place. It's made me wonder..."

"No point holding on to that sort of hope. Ultimately disappoints you."

"Just piss off, you insensitive clown."

10

Robin Hood and Maid Marion

S am was clinging on tightly and he could feel her shaking again. The poor woman had been through the mill in the last few hours, and Kirkgordon reckoned she must be reaching the limit of what a normal person could take. He, however, had long since given up the idea of being a normal person.

As he pretended to be deeply engrossed in caressing Sam's neck, he saw the red headed woman beside him begin to stare at them. She then sniffed the air. This wasn't looking good.

"You have a fear about you, I can smell it. And I can smell my sister on him. Where is she? What have you done with her?"

Pushing Sam behind him, Kirkgordon took up a defensive stance. His arm opened and a bolt was displayed on the small crossbow that emerged.

"You dare to threaten us, from the Romanian High blood? Kneel and we may yet spare you. Where is she?"

Kirkgordon stood his ground and showed a stolid face while his mind panicked about the best option. "She tried and failed to take me. I doubt you'll fare any better." Kirkgordon reckoned if he could keep them talking, the elevator would open and then they would be less likely to try anything.

"Keep up that tone, and I will dispose of your slave." The redheaded vampire hissed as she made the threat.

Kirkgordon felt an arm pushing him to one side and Sam pushed past. "Slave, did that cow just say slave? Who the hell do you think you are? Do you think he owns me? I'm not like you!" Sam had stepped forward and was now pointing a finger under the vampire's chin. "They might own you back at the harem, but here in the normal world, we women are equals. Tell her, tell her what women are to you."

The surrealness of the situation wasn't lost on Kirkgordon, as he was called on to defend his principals of equality whilst carefully watching whether these vampires were about to lunge. Sam was certainly feisty and while Kirkgordon was all for any woman he liked to be of her own mind, right now he was hoping Sam would shut up and get behind him before this all kicked off.

"I don't own her," he ventured, "but I'll fight for her like she's mine if you touch her." He saw Sam's glance to him realising in her eyes he had gone over and above, he also saw the move by the male vampire when she turned her head. As the vampire reached for Sam's throat, Kirkgordon roared and fired a bolt which pinned the creature's hand to the wall of the elevator.

The female vampire shrieked and grabbed Sam by the arm, and Kirkgordon then fired to pin the leg of the redhead to the elevator. As he grabbed Sam and pulled her back, he saw the male vampire pull his arm from the wall and bare his teeth. The redhead shrieked and Kirkgordon, shouting "flame", backed Sam into the corner of the elevator and held a flaming bolt in check aimed at the vampires.

"I'll burn you both to oblivion."

The elevator then sounded a ding and the doors opened. Looking past the vampires, Kirkgordon could see that there was a man there in formal evening dress, looking pale, almost white. But a glance at the mirrored wall of the elevator showed no such person. *Damn!*

"Halt, we have her. Back to the cabin with both of you." Kirkgordon watched the male vampire whom he had tagged, examine his wounded arm and scowl. The redhead glared at Sam and hissed before walking out. After their departure, the vampire who had ordered them out entered the elevator and studied Kirkgordon and Sam. He sniffed the air.

"You," he said pointing at Kirkgordon, "you met her and survived. Next time you will not be so lucky. I will keep her in our quarters, you keep away from us and we shall leave without further incident on our arrival in port. Your woman would not last, so keep her away." With that, he turned on his heel but then stopped and spun back. "And tell Austerley that Count Crupescu will see any intervention as an act of war, and we shall rip through the ship."

Kirkgordon watched closely and something occurred to him. "You're scared of him. You're actually scared of him. Why threaten the ship? Earlier you only threatened me, but when you thought of Austerley, you threatened the entire ship."

The vampire was clearly shaken, but he rallied, "Don't underestimate us with your…"

"No!" roared Kirkgordon, "you shut up and listen. You lay a finger on anyone on this ship, and I'll let Austerley off the leash. No holds barred, and he'll send you to whatever hell or heaven you fear. Don't mess with me. You go back to your cabin. Leave it and you won't leave this ship aliv…, intact."

The vampire narrowed his eyes and then left.

Sam grabbed Kirkgordon around the waist and hung on tight, but Kirkgordon swore. "Alive, I mean alive. Threatening a vampire with not being alive. Bloody hell. I sounded such an arse."

"We lived. Shut up!" And Sam kissed him deep and long. When they broke off, they were both breathing heavily and Kirkgordon broke the moment by suggesting they go back to the cabin, to see Austerley. It seemed that Sam didn't want to leave his side and she took his hand as they left the elevator.

The hours of the early morning saw few people about the passenger quarters and Kirkgordon was glad of the lack of incident during their walk back to the cabin. Obviously still shaken, Sam was gripping his hand like it would fall off and despite telling himself that she was just grateful for being alive, he felt a deep fondness for the woman. After the struggles of Alana and her madness, Calandra's heartbreak and departure and even Tania's penchant for witchery and mayhem, Kirkgordon was enjoying someone simple. No, simple was the wrong word. Someone straight forward, and fun. Sam was definitely fun.

But there was a job to do and he thought about the loose packets he carried and whether Austerley would make anything of them. There were also the stolen sheets from Dr Howard's room. The sooner they understood what was happening and whether the doctor was a threat, then the sooner he could wrap things up and enjoy a holiday. Heck, it would be nice if work would go away and he could spend some time in the company of someone like Sam without any hassles. But there were the kids to think of as well. There wasn't enough time, ever.

As they approached the more salubrious cabins close to Kirkgordon's, Sam's face clearly lit up.

"How do you afford one of these? I had to scrimp to get a balcony, never mind something closer to a small apartment."

Kirkgordon laughed. "It's the company that paid. And the real apartments are a deck or two up. They really are something although I could get used to the pad they gave us. I warn you though, I'm sharing with a work colleague and he's not the most straightforward. So just take it easy around him and don't be offended."

"Why do you think I would get offended?"

"Vampire, finger pointing at him? There's an undead creature with you in their sights and you take offense at his lack of diversity with regard to women. I mean he may have bitten you, turned you and ultimately made you his slave but dammit if he wasn't going to understand your rights before that happened."

Sam laughed. It was slightly nervous as she realised the craziness of what she had done. "Still, I had my Robin Hood. Marion was always safe."

Kirkgordon stopped in his tracks and turned her to face him. "Look Sam, this isn't a movie. There isn't just a load of near scrapes and then we all laugh and wind up in a Jacuzzi with the job done. I've lost people, dead and not in pleasant ways. Had friends scarred and torn. And I've basically lost my wife to all purposes as she's gone mad with a form of possession. Understand if I didn't think you were under threat, I would not have brought you with me. Now the vampires have seen you, now that you basically insulted them and threatened them, because of this, I am keeping you with me. By choice, I'd keep you away from it, you're too good to be tainted by this nonsense I am involved in."

"But here we are." Sam reached up and pulled his face to her. Kissing him gently, she then broke into a smile.

"Stay close. And no insulting anything that's not human." They both laughed. And Kirkgordon wished he could just put her somewhere on hold until this job was done, somewhere safe so he could pick it all back up afterwards in a quiet time. He knew the scars would come, deeper than those she had suffered already in the short time she'd been exposed to this strange world he now inhabited.

Walking on, the air felt charged, a tension, an excitement that came with not knowing each other but a desperation to find out. But also a thought that something will break it all up sooner rather than later. But he knew his weakness was once again surfacing. He'd stand all day against the hordes of hell, but a half caring, interested woman could march straight through his defences any day.

At the cabin door, he made Sam stand behind him, and he slid the key card through the slot. He pushed the cabin door open to find his arm grabbed, and he was dragged through the door. Going with his opponent's move, he was able to spin around and grab an arm and rotate behind and forced the woman attacking him to the floor, jamming her arm behind her back.

"Austerley? Are you with Austerley?"

"Mr Kirkgordon, let my arm go," said the woman who had attacked him. "I think you have made your point. Mr Austerley is in the bedroom." The woman turned her head and Kirkgordon gazed straight into her eyes. Then he saw the elegance of her chin, the cheek bones and her tidy hair. Just

66

like a female…

"You're a Havers? Where's Austerley?"

A shambling hulk in one of the loudest shirts ever seen came out of the bedroom and stared at Sam who had followed Kirkgordon into the room. Austerley looked her up and down before tutting.

"Another bloody woman. Are you some sort of addict?"

Kirkgordon nodded at the woman held in an arm lock at his feet. "Touché, Austerley, flaming touché!"

11

Debriefs

"It's not like you wouldn't have seen our pictures. I think you might have recognised me," said Kirkgordon.

"You left Mr Austerley, it could have been anyone coming through that door," Hannah retorted.

"But it wasn't, you don't just go gung-ho at whoever is arriving, what sort of an operative are you?"

"Clerical, research, basic assistance in the field. Not a protection operative and certainly not a babysitter like you."

"She's actually quite intelligent," interjected Austerley. "I mean, reasonably so."

"Well, with compliments like that…" retorted Hannah.

"And why does no one tell me who's on my side?" raged Kirkgordon. "And for your information, Austerley can look after himself."

"Possibly," the female agent responded, "But we have to protect the general public from him."

"Can I just go and make some drinks because people seem to be getting a little stressed?" Everyone turned and looked at Sam who had been quiet until this time. Running a loose hand down Kirkgordon's back, she made her way to the kettle and filled it up with water.

"Anyway, Indy," continued Kirkgordon, "I got you some info on the camera, here." Austerley caught the small device tossed to him and made his way to a laptop sat on the desk in the cabin. Slotting the camera's USB into the side of the laptop, he waited for the pictures to appear. Sam smiled at Kirkgordon from the other end of the room. At least that was something, she now seemed calmer and relaxed. The last thing he needed was for her to go crazy and panicky.

"I also found this," said Kirkgordon, throwing the small, mainly empty packets he found on the cargo hold.

"Looks empty."

"Well thanks, Indy, of course they are empty. It's from Dr Howard's stash in the cargo bay but they have moved it. This was all that remained. Can you tell what it is?"

Austerley stuck a finger into the bag and sucked on it. "Well, possibilities, but I reckon the powder here is the carrier for the active ingredient. I'll need to test it."

"Okay, but get cracking on it as if they have moved it, they are probably about to use it."

Sam brought a steaming cup of tea to Kirkgordon, and he gratefully took it but was surprised when she cuddled into him. After a hard squeeze, she broke off to return to her task of giving drinks to everyone.

"I'm going to need to sleep, Austerley, but you get cracked on working out that manuscript and the powder."

"Do you to want to know what I discovered?"

Part of Kirkgordon didn't, he just wanted his bed. But the professional part insisted on hearing him out. Austerley told of the rumours of a city beneath the waves being correct, with references of how many times it had been seen. He had also read that there existed a document with directions to the city and a method of raising it. And that within this city was a power to be tapped and used to restore things, but also to create self-destructive things. It was Austerley's considered opinion that this power was Dr Howard's goal and the assassin they had discovered was trying to stop the city ever being discovered. But Austerley still didn't know exactly where to find the city nor how to make it rise.

The documents brought back by Kirkgordon seemed to be in code and Austerley suggested that Hannah work on them while he worked on the powders in the bags from the cargo hold. Nodding vaguely, Kirkgordon entered his bedroom and lay down exhausted. A knock followed shortly.

"Come in."

"Were you wanting me to do anything in particular?" Sam stood questioningly at the door.

"Oh, sorry. Just too tired. Can't think."

"Well then, I'll make a decision then," and Sam closed the door behind her and promptly took off her top and leggings without any fuss. Kirkgordon watched her approach the bed in her underwear and she began to remove his trousers. Part of him said he should just tell her to stop but frankly, he didn't want her to. Now in just his t-shirt and underwear, he watched her pull the sheets down from under him before covering him up again.

"Turn over," Sam commanded.

Unsure as to what was coming next, he did as instructed. He heard her walk to the light switch, saw the lights go dark and then heard her remove the cover behind him and climb into the bed. The touch of her flesh on his gave a warmth he had missed in recent times, and he happily received two hungry arms around him. A kiss followed on his back.

"Get no ideas, I'm here to sleep. But I need someone close, someone to protect me. So just do that. You hear…"

But there were only snores from the weary protector.

*****

The door almost broke its hinges due to the force of the knocking. And then there was a tap on his back. Kirkgordon started but then remembered where he was.

"I think it's time to get up. We should get some dinner," came Hannah's voice.

"Well, I need a shower," whispered Sam. Without any obvious embarrassment, she climbed out of bed and dropped her underwear to the floor. Watching her cross to the bathroom, Kirkgordon was mesmerized and only the bathroom door closing caused him to respond to Hannah.

"Yeah, okay. Did you say dinner?"

"Yes, dinner. It's almost seven o'clock."

Twelve hours, almost twelve hours, thought Kirkgordon. *I was exhausted.* He rolled out of bed and grabbed a t-shirt from his drawer. Walking through to the main room of the cabin, he saw Hannah at work on the laptop and Austerley looking smug in a chair in the corner, watching Hannah.

"Have you guys found anything?"

"Zombies," said Austerley.

"What? Zombies? First vampires and now zombies."

"Yes, but not the neuro-obsessive necrosis that you would be familiar with."

"I would?"

"This is more mind control, suggestibility, getting someone to do your will. The substances I found are used in a

71

Haitian ritual to control someone's mind, making them highly suggestible to the point that they could be advised to kill, which they would do without hesitation."

"Indy, are you for real?"

"Yes, he very much is," said Hannah. "The practice is a long and ancient one, but the real question is why does he want to zombify people? And who?"

"And what did the papers I stole say?"

"Well, in summary," continued Hannah, "they were a brief explanation of how to get to the sunken city he's looking for. It also reinforced the idea that there is a power source there. But the exact location and how to get there are unknown as you didn't get the whole manuscript."

"There were a lot of papers and no time. Being in code didn't help either."

"Anyway," said Austerley, "I need some food so let's go have dinner. I've booked us a table at the posh restaurant as that's probably where Dr Howard or his associates will eat. At least that's what Hannah has heard."

"Good, I'll go get changed then. You joining us Hannah?"

"Hardly, I'm crew. I was back and forward to my day job while you slept."

"Of course. Better get ready, Indy." Kirkgordon turned away back towards his room. He thought he should knock but then heard the shower still running. Once inside his bedroom, he closed the door and then knocked on the en-suite.

"Just a minute."

Kirkgordon waited.

"Is there a towel?"

Kirkgordon looked at the towels from the bathroom that were lying in the corner of the room. Finding the driest one, he announced that he had one and would throw it inside. The door swung open and Sam was standing, fully exposed, before him with her hair dripping down her front. She stood awaiting the towel but then grabbed it when she found that Kirkgordon had become a silent statue. Laughing, she rubbed herself down without any attempt to conceal.

"Your first woman?" she mocked.

"Sorry, it's been a while. Wow! I mean that, wow!"

"Shut up and get in the shower." Brushing past him, she gave a small kiss to his cheek. Almost instinctively, he pulled her in and kissed her back more strongly, more deeply. When he let go, she smiled before saying, "You, shower."

Kirkgordon nodded and started up the shower again. "By the way, Sam, unless you want to stay here, we're going to dinner, with Austerley. It's a scouting job, nothing social. But if you'd rather not, I can give you an alarm and you can rest up here." There was no answer.

When he emerged from the shower Sam was still in the towel lying on the bed with the television on. Her bare legs were exposed, and she watched Kirkgordon closely as he went to change. Assuming she wasn't coming, he changed and tried to smarten up in a tuxedo. Classical, black and white, he felt like a strung up bird.

"Here," said Kirkgordon. "If there's trouble just press that alarm, and I'll come running." Sam seemed distant, so he repeated the statement.

"Sorry. I was just seeing that vampire's face again."

"It's okay. You don't get used to this stuff."

"I said I wanted some fun but this doesn't feel so much like that. Well, except for you."

"Well that's a start. I'll try and be quick. And no soaps on

73

that television. Do you need clothes brought over?"

"Food would be good."

"Order room service."

"No, I ain't opening the door to anyone."

And he saw the fear in her eyes. So he didn't mention what Austerley had found out. Nothing about hidden power or zombification. If she gets all this at once, she'll go crazy like Austerley.

"Okay, I'll bring something back. But no soaps."

12

The Absurdity of Beverage Generosity

The Starlight Grill was impressive with its glass roof showing off the night sky and a sea view from the higher deck that basically showed endless ocean at this time. Kirkgordon imagined that being in port or tracing a coastline must be spectacular while you eat your dinner. The company could also be better, he thought, having been stuck with Austerley. Nonetheless, they were fortunate enough to be afforded a small table and not a large social table that could accommodate twelve people, and so many strangers. This was recon and he wanted some privacy.

From their vantage point, they could see the top table where the Master of the ship was dining with some special guests and amongst them were Dr Howard and his female associate. He was dressed in a smart black and white tuxedo, like Kirkgordon, but the tailoring looked about ten times the price of Kirkgordon's. And the woman wore a snappy, green cocktail dress that looked very business-like.

"I can't see any assassins, Churchy."

"No, Indy, they tend to try and hide themselves."

Austerley threw him a dirty look. "I don't see anyone unusual with them either. No vampires certainly, and trust me they would be here. They really must be staying in for the night. There's no way they could resist this type of occasion. That's the thing with the higher ones, they are so steeped in occasion."

"They still seem to want to kill people. I don't see the fascination in them. Just monsters."

"Well," said Austerley, "that's what people would have said about Khan, Alexander the Great, most Roman emperors but once you understand the times and the issues, you begin to appreciate how they operate and how…"

They were interrupted by a waiter with a trim but substantial beard who was offering a wine list. He spoke in broken English and seemed to be Spanish in origin.

"Wine. You like wine, gentleman. I can bring you wine, if you pick here, si?"

Austerley grabbed the list and began perusing it.

"Just water, please," said Kirkgordon, "Waiter, look at me, we just need a water. From the tap."

"Si, señor, I get you two waters."

With that, the waiter disappeared and Austerley swore. "I wanted wine. If I'm going to have to sit here and study these people I might as well have enjoyed a good merlot, or even a rioja. I don't want water."

"It's okay, I need to hydrate. You can talk to him when he comes back."

Austerley went into a mood, but Kirkgordon felt himself beginning to fidget and purposefully calmed himself down. There was something about the waiter, in the midst of all this stunning theatre that was the restaurant. Something wasn't right, but he had dealt mainly with Austerley and so he hadn't got to really look. But he would when the waiter came back. *Faces, I don't forget faces. But especially eyes. Eyes that hold hate and anger, the biggest giveaways. Faces that hold an outer facade but when you look closer, you see the fire burning.*

While he was waiting for his water, Kirkgordon noticed that several bottles of wine were being distributed amongst the guests. Another waiter left three bottles on their table quickly, before depositing more on other tables. Taking one of the bottles, Kirkgordon checked the label. It was a red wine, merlot apparently.

"Indy, is this good?"

"Blimey, that's something else, probably about £30 a bottle that one."

"And it's being given away."

"These cruises do cost a bomb. I doubt it would cost that much in the grand scheme of things. Anyway, something to have now."

Kirkgordon put his hand on the bottle. "No! Later you can, but not while we are watching them. I need you sober and ready if something kicks off." He saw Austerley roll his eyes. "Maybe you can share a bottle with that Hannah later."

Austerley looked at him, almost angry. "I don't think you should talk about my contact with women. I ain't the one who has a woman in his room, an angel left in tears because she can't be with you and a wife in a sanatorium. Every woman you come into contact with suffers, you should be neutered for the good of womankind."

"Hold on, you pompous ass, you got me into the madness that ruined my wife, you were just jealous about Cally, and as for Sam, just leave it. She's scared, and I'm keeping her safe."

"Of course. I protect all my maidens in distress by showering them in my bathroom, have them wandering around in a towel, and then sleeping with them."

"So she's interested. And anyway we didn't sleep together. We only shared the same bed."

He saw Austerley go to speak and shot a look that threatened physical action. However, the subsequent silence seemed to accuse him. *What is it with me and women? I don't try to stray, in fact I haven't strayed! I never did with Cally, and God knows I wanted to. And as for Alana, well she's not there. She's no longer the woman she ever was. And Sam's only a bit of fun. She said as much. Whatever that is.*

Wrapped up in his own thoughts he almost missed the waiter coming back with his water. He was quick, almost too quick. He placed Austerley's water first smiling at him before turning and placing Kirkgordon's glass on the table without looking at him. Kirkgordon took a monetary note from his pocket and called the waiter. The man turned and put up a finger indicating no, but he also looked at Kirkgordon.

No way. It can't be. How did he survive? What's he doing here? That's a stupid question, if he's here with that fire in his eyes then it must mean Farthington's... How are they alive?

"Please, take the money," Kirkgordon said to the waiter. "Or should I just leave it here, on the platform? Be careful, in case it slides off."

The waiter shook his finger and turned away. Raising his head, Austerley looked quizzical.

"Platform. I think he might have understood table, after all it's what they are doing here. I imagine he can say it in French, or German. Maybe other languages too. As for tempting him

78

to get it before you let it fall…and you call me a bastard."

"How can you be so clever and miss stuff right in front of your face? You know that waiter. And what's more, if he's here things may be getting a little more complicated."

"What man? How do I know him, he's just a Spanish waiter? Looks like all the rest."

"Ignoring your blatantly racist comment, he does not look like all the rest. In fact, I think he could look like anyone he wanted to. But he can't hide the eyes or the purposefulness, Mr Austerley."

"No," Austerley blurted out before hushing his voice. "He sailed off that platform. I told Hannah so. He's gone, gone to wherever but he's gone. Along with that bastard Farthington. You saw it."

"I saw them slide off the platform. I never saw where they went. I don't know where he's been but wherever it was, he has been after Farthington. And what's more, he's here."

There was a commotion and then a tapping of glasses. The room fell silent as the ship's master stood up and addressed everyone. He thanked the benefactor who had provided the wine given to every passenger, and indeed to the crew, and asked everyone to hold a glass aloft and drink a toast.

"More like it," said Austerley, "we need to stay in cover so I'm having some."

"No!" Kirkgordon cut in. "See how everyone's getting a glass, even the crew? But that Spanish waiter isn't taking a glass. He's lifted some water instead. Don't you touch a drop. Raise the water. Just raise the water."

The whole restaurant raised a glass and drank down. Kirkgordon waited for something. But everyone carried on with their conversations and enjoyment. Another night of enjoyment on board the cruise ship was underway.

"Well, that was splendid. Best bit of wine I'm likely to have in the near future, and I can't have it."

Kirkgordon stood up. "We're going. Howard is leaving anyway, he's made some sort of excuse. And bring those bottles. You need to check them."

"Oh, I'll taste them alright."

"Analytically, Indy."

*****

The boys returned to the cabin without incident, and Kirkgordon looked forward to seeing Sam. Hannah was in the cabin when they got there, sipping tea and working on some of the sheets Kirkgordon had brought back from Dr Howard's quarters.

"Is Sam asleep?" asked Kirkgordon.

"She wasn't feeling too great, went to bed feeling hot. I think she's possibly in the shower again although it's a bit strange as she's been in twice from what I have heard."

Kirkgordon knocked his bedroom door but turned when Austerley shouted for him. From the far side of the room, he held up a bottle, the same as was served at the restaurant. The bottle was empty.

"Did you have any of that Hannah?" asked Austerley.

"No, just Sam. I think she was feeling the pace with all that's happened, so drunk her sorrows. The bottle was empty when I got here. But they have been handing those out to everyone. Quite pushy with it actually."

"And Sam's had a bucketful." Kirkgordon's voice was agitated. He turned and opened his bedroom door. There was no one in the room. The bed was a mess like someone had been tossing and turning. The shower wasn't on, but he felt the moisture from it having been used recently, in the air.

"Sam? Where are you Sam? It's me. It's fine, it's just me, you can come out."

There was a grunt from the bathroom and something smashed. His heart now racing, Kirkgordon grabbed the handle and pulled the door open. Something jumped on him. As he fell back on the ground, he saw a wild and furious Sam lash out at him, scraping long sharp nails across his face. The blood spattered into her white bathrobe, and she swung hard with her other hand.

13

Innocent Zombies

O n instinct, Kirkgordon blocked the hand swung at him and tried not to focus on the eyes filled with venom. Because he was prone on his back, he was struggling to get any traction to throw Sam off, and he found himself fending off repeated blows. The other thing that was becoming apparent was the incredible strength she seemed to possess. It was like every muscle in her body was on overdrive.

Hannah came racing through the door of the bedroom and tried to grab Sam's shoulders in an effort to haul her off. A sharp elbow caught Hannah on the chin, and she reeled backwards clattering into the wall. Austerley came behind and stood looking at the situation with an almost quizzical look on his face.

"Don't just stand there, Indy, get her off me! Shift your arse!"

With Austerley standing motionless, Kirkgordon decided to take matters in hand. He grabbed Sam's left wrist as the hand swung at him and then trapped the right wrist as she countered. Holding both hands apart he stared into Sam's eyes and failed to see the woman he had started to get close to.

Sure, her body was the same, bathrobe carelessly covering her curves, but the face was contorted and savage. But he thought he felt the tide turning as he pushed back on her wrists and began to force her upwards.

"That's it, girl, let's just calm down."

Sam nutted him with a sudden explosion of force. His head hammered onto the floor behind him, and he struggled to do anything. He felt a pounding on his chest and then nothing. There was the sound of a body hitting the floor, and he tried to focus. It seemed Sam had been taken care of. Extricating himself from under her body, Kirkgordon sought the source of this action. Austerley was the only person still standing.

"How? What did you do?"

"What you do," grinned Austerley. "I may not have your speed but I have plenty of experience of being nerve pinched to oblivion, thanks mainly to yourself, and well, the actual nerve strike isn't that difficult. You just have to hit the right bit. You had her distracted, so I hit the nerve."

"How hard? Austerley, how hard? I can kill with a nerve strike."

"It was from me, so I doubt it was anything like that hard. I mean look, she's still breathing."

Kirkgordon took Sam in his arms and laid her on the bed. Carefully he wrapped her robe around her, covering her naked parts. He reached into his drawers and pulled out some duct tape and rope and began to bind Sam up tightly.

"I'm alright guys. I mean don't mind me. Just take care of the half-naked, mad woman." Hannah was getting groggily to her feet.

"You're not like your cousin," said Austerley.

"Wow, Indy, make her feel good. Are you okay, Hannah?

Thanks for trying."

"Yeah, I've been clobbered before. But that was a hell of an elbow. Where did she get that strength from?"

"I'm not sure," said Austerley, his face contorting as he thought. "The powders you found would certainly make people become zombie like, open to suggestion but there's been no announcement, no gathering together for a purpose. Normally to make a subject your slave via this method you would need to have them in your grasp and almost hypnotise them while the drugs were taking effect. And the subject would be incredibly slow, almost dull witted."

"But she was sharp," answered Kirkgordon. "Extremely fast, I would say enhanced. And her strength was incredible for her frame."

"If you need to hypnotically install a control," interjected Hannah, "is there anything to say it can't be done sublimi-nally?"

"Good thinking. But it would need to be something every-one would see." Austerley smiled at Hannah and Kirkgordon saw he was impressed with her in more ways than one.

"That sounds very complicated," ventured Kirkgordon. "I mean the drinks were given out to everyone, crew included. That means it would need to be something everyone would read."

"No," said Hannah, "you could have multiple instructions, that way you could reach everyone."

"Yes," agreed Austerley, "then you would get everyone. Have there been any recent ship's notices that all crew have to read."

Hannah nodded. "It's fairly normal to have those. There was an innocuous one about carpeting."

"No," said Kirkgordon. "Something safety based, one you

84

cannot ignore."

"Oh yes, there was a safety drill that actually stated to be read by all and section heads to make sure everyone had."

"Bingo!" said Kirkgordon.

"And for passengers, there's the joining instructions you receive. Even if only half read that, you'll have over half the ship as zombies. Probably enough to do whatever it is he wants."

"He wants the sunken city and the power that comes with it. It has to be that," said Austerley.

There came a bang on the door of the cabin. It was followed by successive loud crashes. Indicating to Hannah to keep an eye on Sam, Kirkgordon raced to the main cabin door to find a foot sticking through it. As he got closer a fist drove another hole in the solid panelling. Kirkgordon grabbed the door handle and swung it open. A middle aged man with a wild look on his face hung on the door as it opened and Kirkgordon nerve pinched him. Grabbing the man by the scruff of the neck, he flung him off the door and shut it. Down the corridor he could hear screams.

"Austerley, it's spreading. I just had a zombie trying to break in. I doubt the cabin will be safe for too long. Where's the best place to go? We need to hide up and think how we are going to stop this."

"Hannah," asked Austerley, as Kirkgordon re-entered the bedroom, "where's good? Where do they have solid lockable doors?"

"Mind, it can't be a hole with no escape route out the back," advised Kirkgordon. "If we get a thousand zombies at the door I doubt we'll fight our way out."

"The ship's safe. There's a strong room where we could go

if the ship was attacked by pirates. Actually there's a few, but the nearest to here is in crew quarters. Down ten decks and in the centre of the ship."

"Does it have a back way out?" asked Kirkgordon.

"I don't know."

"And Indy, is this condition reversible?"

Kirkgordon was almost pleading but Austerley remained his usual aloof self. "Unknown. Normal zombification wouldn't be that difficult, but he's done this in a fashion I'm not familiar with. So who's to say?"

"Bloody great. Come on." Kirkgordon swept Sam into his arms.

"Hang on," said Hannah. "You're the strongest fighter we have, why are you carrying her?"

"It's fine," said Kirkgordon, his arm opening up to reveal the crossbow, "I'll get rid of anyone in front of us."

"Like that?" Hannah was horrified. "These are people, innocent people. We can't just kill them off. We need to undo this. Until that time, we have to keep safe and not kill everyone else!"

Knowing she was right, Kirkgordon placed Sam back onto the bed. "Well, Austerley won't be able to carry her. And he's quite handy in a fight if he's given space. Are you able to carry her, Hannah?"

Hannah nodded and lifted Sam up onto her shoulder. It was clear that it wasn't comfortable, but the agent was refusing any help.

"Remember, we can't stop for others yet. We need to get to safety and then see if Austerley can find a cure. We've got Sam to work on. If we stop, we may never get anywhere." Kirkgordon quickly changed into his combat gear and armed

86

himself. He took a rucksack and packed what he could find of Sam's clothes, throwing in the notes Austerley and Hannah had been working on. Lastly, he grabbed some bottles of water and then rounded his team up. Hannah again took on the burden of Sam and placed herself between Kirkgordon and Austerley.

"One last thing," said Kirkgordon and took an alerter from his jacket. "I think we may need help, this should bring HQ after us." Hannah smiled at the news. *Yes*, thought Kirkgordon, *could do with Cally, Nefol, Scarlett and Wilson. This is much bigger than I thought. Well, certainly more people than I reckoned.*

Alerter activated, Kirkgordon strode to the door and opened it. A raging face of a young man met him and was then introduced to Kirkgordon's forehead as he nutted him to the floor. Stepping out, he dodged an assailant and quickly struck a nerve in the back of the neck.

"Okay, let's move out. It's fairly quiet here but it might not be further up. Indy, any problems at the rear, just shout."

The peculiar party moved down the salubrious corridor, past broken doors. Inside a few were frightened faces, people who hadn't or were yet to be affected. It felt unnatural leaving them behind, but Kirkgordon knew he couldn't keep a large party safe at this time. It was a hard-hearted decision, but it was the only viable one. Who knew what these zombies were capable of?

A door smashed apart just after Kirkgordon walked past it. A hand reached out and grabbed Hannah, pulling her into the room. Sam fell from her shoulder to the floor, still bound and Austerley froze before the door.

"Move!" yelled Kirkgordon and pushed Austerley aside. Hannah was being held by a massive man, possibly from the

South Seas, given his skin colour and tattoos. He had her by the neck and was seemingly about to bite into her neck.

Dropping to one knee, he called for his cross bow which promptly erupted from his arm. Without hesitation, he fired a bolt into the man's clear shoulder and saw him whip off his feet. Hannah stumbled away as she was released and Kirkgordon grabbed her and dragged her from the room. But the noise inside had caused more zombies in the locale to hone in on their position.

Exiting the room, Kirkgordon saw their way blocked by a horde down the corridor and picked Sam off the floor. "Run! Back the way we came!"

When he heard his colleagues were following him, he counted to five as he ran. Then he stopped and turned. "Flame." With his arm held up he fired a burning bolt into some plush curtains which erupted into flame. The zombies half panicked and seemed confused, almost like they couldn't see beyond the flames.

"Fascinating," said Austerley, "it must change the colour perception of the eye, so it becomes base. Like a chicken and red or green for food. The flame must speak of danger or void or something. Just fascinating."

"Indy," called Kirkgordon racing up the corridor, "would you fascinate your arse this way!"

Kirkgordon was aware he was still in the region of his cabin and hadn't gotten far but then it occurred that he was also near to a cabin he certainly didn't want to go into. As he approached where the door to the cabin was, he saw it had been breached, shattered into many pieces. But there were no noises from inside. Carefully he poked his head around the door and saw a cabin with two coffins inside. The lids were off. *Oh shit!*

There was a yell from the corridor ahead and Kirkgordon thought about running the other direction but there was something to the cry. Something that resonated in that voice. Racing around the corner, Sam still over his shoulder, he saw a waiter with a beard standing motionless and with his head tilted to one side. Before him stood a cloaked figure, pale as the moon. And with bloody fangs.

From behind him, he heard Hannah scream. "Arthur!"

14

The Return of Major Havers

"Unhand him, now!" cried Kirkgordon. Standing with Sam over his shoulder and a screaming Hannah on his other side, he didn't imagine he carried that much threat, but he had an ace up his sleeve.

"I thought I said to leave us alone! Zombies, human zombies at that, frauds of the undead. You dare to disturb our sleep with these shambolic excuse for creature. No, we shall take this vessel for ourselves, and this man before me shall just be another." The eyes of the vampire before him seemed to burn into his mind and he knew he should show his cards quickly.

"Austerley!" The vampire stopped suddenly and Kirkgordon swore he saw fear there. The proud attitude fell slightly as the creature scanned for the dreaded Austerley. Lurching from behind, Kirkgordon's colleague stumbled onto the scene puffing and panting in the limpest arrival of a hero he had ever witnessed.

"You! They have spoken of you. The Romanian hive, every single one of them. But then they were Krystakovs, not a true blood line like we are. You will not have dealt with royalty before."

Austerley coughed. Then he coughed again. "Dammit, I need a drink. Oh, that was a bit of a run. Right, the Krystakovs, took about two hours. Every one of them, village unbothered since. And..., sorry just a minute..., I've got your measure. Go back to the coffins, go rest and I'll stand down. Let us sort this mess, and you'll get to your destination safely."

"You must think me a fool. Look around you, even if we did retire, there would be an investigation on what happened here. We would be discovered. No, we need to take charge, and we will, Professor Austerley, so stand back or be destroyed." The vampire turned back to the entranced man in front of him and Hannah broke rank and ran towards the vampire.

"No!" yelled Kirkgordon, "Indy, do something."

From behind his back, Austerley pulled out a wooden cross, barely larger than a man's hand. He turned to Kirkgordon and handed it to him before lifting Sam onto his own shoulder.

"Just go at him. It'll drive him away."

"Me?" asked Kirkgordon, "Why me? Shouldn't you do it?"

"Where do you think the power comes from? It'll be stronger in your hands."

Kirkgordon wasn't fully understanding Austerley but regardless he stuck his arm out in front of him and walked towards the vampire. At first there seemed to be no effect but then the creature turned. Spitting blasphemies out loud, it focused on the cross.

Another voice spoke. "You really think that can stop us? There's no trust here, no faith to back up the symbol's bold claims. You have no faith, Professor. You never have, and I doubt you ever will. There's no power that'll hold against me."

"You're right," shouted Austerley to the unseen voice. "I

don't have faith. It would be weak in my hands. That's why it's in his."

Kirkgordon had continued his march towards the vampire, and it was now throwing its arms up to shield itself. Amazed, Kirkgordon watched the side of the vampire suddenly begin to smoulder in the shape of a cross. The vampire howled and suddenly exploded into a dark fog. As Kirkgordon arrived at the spot where the vampire had stood, he saw the fog disappear down the corridor.

"Good," said Austerley. "At last you're useful."

Hannah was beside the waiter with the beard who was slowly coming around from the trance state he had been in.

"Arthur, are you there? Arthur! Snap out of it." She slapped him across the face. And again, harder. When she attempted a third slap, a hand flew up and caught her at the wrist.

"I think that's enough, my dear. My, my, imagine running into family out here. You're looking well."

"Arthur, thank God." Hannah flung her arms around him and then planted a kiss on his forehead.

"It is a joy to see you, trust me Hannah, it is. But for the sake of having more moments like this, may I suggest we retire somewhere safer. Ah, you have help too, excellent. Mr Austerley, and the outstanding Mr Kirkgordon, team leader extraordinaire."

"Havers, ton of questions here but no time. We're headed for the safe room decks below. I could use a point man. Are you fully functional?"

"For Queen and friends, always. Let us hasten then. Which way?"

"Hannah, lead the way with the Major," said Kirkgordon, noting Havers nod at Kirkgordon's use of his title. "I'll get

Sam, and Austerley can bring up the rear."

"Sam?" queried Havers and then concluded it must be the woman on Austerley's shoulder. "I see your penchant for collecting women continues, Mr Kirkgordon. In that respect, I dare say even Romeo would be jealous."

Kirkgordon let the comment drop and took Sam from Austerley's shoulder. "Okay, let's roll."

"Wait," said Austerley. "These vampires are out now and angry. They won't be tamed, and we'll have to deal with them at some point. But as we are here and we have frightened them off for the meantime, we should destroy their resting place."

"Right now?" asked Kirkgordon.

"He's right, Mr Kirkgordon. It'll be a place to come back to and recharge. It'll also force them to hide when the daylight comes, unable to have a safe place."

Looking up and down the corridor in apprehension, Kirkgordon eventually nodded. "Okay, we all retire into their cabin. Then I want you on guard duty, Havers. Hannah you can help Austerley with destroying whatever is in there, and I'll guard the balcony. They climb the sides of ships."

"My goodness, we are becoming knowledgeable, Mr Kirkgordon, but your plan is sound."

"No," said Austerley. "I need Churchy."

"Me? Why?"

"Because I need a Churchy."

Kirkgordon shook his shoulders but followed Austerley into the cabin of the vampires. Given how quickly and calmly Austerley was working, Kirkgordon reasoned he must have known it was clear. In the cabin which was as extensive as Dr Howard's, there were two large and ornate caskets sitting in the middle of the lounge area. Where the balcony was located, two large blackout curtains had been erected making the room extremely dark, lit only by the dull green light of an emergency exit sign.

Kirkgordon set Sam down on the floor and watched Austerley fill a large bowl of water. From within his garb he also produced a number of small wooden crosses about the size of a coin. Calling Kirkgordon to him, he laid the items and the bowl on a table.

"Bless them."

"What?"

"I said bless them. You know, pray over them," said Austerley.

"Bless them? You need a vicar for that. Or maybe a Catholic?"

"Priesthood of all believers. Do you know nothing about your own faith? It's no wonder it hasn't taken over the world with ignoramuses like you."

"Okay, okay. I don't generally bless things."

"Well, start now."

Kirkgordon muttered a prayer over the top of the items and hoped he looked solemn enough when doing it. A thought came into his head of how the blackness had been removed from his mind in the "Nether Lands", of how things had worked out on the Scottish Island when all was a mess. He did believe in a guiding hand, the hand of his God. It was just with Alana and the way that had gone, he hadn't been on speaking terms much lately.

"Good," said Austerley, and picked up the bowl. He began sprinkling the water all over the caskets before pushing the lids off, revealing a soil covered interior. Again he sprinkled the water and dropped the crosses into the elaborate coffins. He then set off about the cabin throwing water here and there.

He then returned to the main area and began to pull down the blackout curtain. Opening the door to the balcony, he threw water over the outdoor area, before dropping a line of crosses on the floor at the door.

"Okay, I'm done. Would have been better with wolfsbane or garlic, but we have to make do."

"Havers, we move out in two minutes," advised Kirkgordon, taking a bottle of water from the mini bar and downing it quickly. He hoisted Sam back onto his shoulder and thought about how he always seemed to be carrying one of his team around. Maybe he should retire and be a coal delivery man.

The team resumed their journey to the safe room and initially the area seemed clear. However, once they had travelled along two corridors, a lurching figure appeared at the front of the group. It was a middle aged woman who looked slightly overweight but who raced towards them on sight, hissing and spitting with a fury which seemed wholly unnatural.

Havers met her and stepped to one side, grabbed her head and she dropped to the floor motionless. Hannah screamed and turned away from the woman's prone body.

"Havers, don't kill them! These are ordinary people, we don't put them down unless we need to." Kirkgordon stood horrified at Havers actions.

"If they're coming at me, don't be afraid to do that," said Austerley.

"Indy, enough!"

"What makes you think she is dead, Mr Kirkgordon? You're not the only one who can strike nerves. I also have a host of other tricks. And since when did I butcher the innocent?"

Kirkgordon nodded his apology and Havers turned almost

smugly to continue the trip. They were now close to the stairs and the descent to safety. But Kirkgordon was on edge, especially after the vampire encounter. Could they turn people into vampires? Could there be a greater horde formed? And there was still the question of Dr Howard to stop. This first trip was only the beginning.

They came upon the door to the stairs, and Havers held up a hand. Carefully, Kirkgordon set Sam down and joined Havers at the door to the stairs. Peeping through the window, he saw the problem. The stairs were full of zombies, pushing and fighting over each other. Evidently, doors were proving a bigger problem for them on the stairs than at the cabins, where they just smashed through them. Time to find another route.

"Kirkgordon, she's waking." Hannah's face was pale as she spoke. Sam was sitting upright but still bound and was looking around as if she had never seen this place or maybe was trying to work out where she was. Then she saw Austerley and stared right at him.

"Hello, my special friend. The man who sends flames into the water, very clever, but I think you see now you are outnumbered. And now we have control, we shall come for you. Oh yes, I can see you magic man, I can see you." Sam's head turned and looked directly at the deck plan. "Oh yes, I know where you are, little rat. The exterminator is coming. Time to die little rat, time to die."

15

Partings

"They can see us," cried Hannah. She put herself up against the wall, looking desperately up and down the corridor.

"Calm yourself, dear cousin," said Havers.

"Calm, they are after us and you say keep calm?! I'm the brains in the organisation, not a field operative. I was specifically rendezvousing with Professor Austerley for translation and clerical assistance, not here to fight a war!"

"War comes when it wants, we rarely choose to be in it. Calm yourself, Hannah."

"Don't see what you lot are complaining about. It was me they named, me they are coming for," howled Austerley.

"Enough!" yelled Kirkgordon. "As Havers says, stay calm. First actions, Havers?"

"We need to neutralise their advantage."

"Whoa," said Kirkgordon putting up his hands, "you're not killing off anyone, especially Sam."

"Why do you always assume the worst in me? I am merely suggesting that we blindfold and gag your blonde companion.

That way we neutralise their efforts."

"We will still find you. We are coming little rat…"

Sam fell to one side as Kirkgordon gave her a nerve pinch. He hoisted her onto his back and scanned the corridor.

"Indy, can you reverse what's happened to these people?"

"Probably, Churchy, with time and by working on each individual subject. Better to break the cycle at the source. If we take out the head, the one giving commands, there is a strong possibility that they will revert to normal. No guarantees, but that would be the best option."

"Good," said Kirkgordon. "Havers, you're best suited to that, who else do you need?"

"Well, it would help if I knew who I was aiming for. I assume you have some idea?"

"It's Dr Howard and his people. They were at the top table when you served us earlier tonight. He was beside the master of the ship, there were the big guys protecting him and the woman."

"The woman might be the channel," said Austerley. "She's probably the cause. She was recognising me when she was speaking through Sam."

"Good, so she's probably the source," agreed Kirkgordon.

"It's not bloody good, they are coming for me."

"Then, Indy, I suggest we separate you and Havers, let him move about unannounced."

"Good, Mr Kirkgordon, we'll make a leader of you yet, but I suggest we get moving ourselves as they won't take long to get here. Ditch the girl and tie her up somewhere. You can come back for her when the battle's over."

"No, Havers, they know she's one of us, if they get her, they can use her as blackmail. She's staying with me."

"The woman of the world must feel so much safer knowing there's such chivalry as your own, Mr Kirkgordon. I'll take Hannah with me, she'll be safe, and I need a guide on this vessel. I didn't have time to take in any schematics."

"Good, I'll guess we'll see the effects if you are successful."

"Keep the bug hunt going as long as you can, Mr Kirkgordon. I will see you soon."

Kirkgordon watched Havers grab his cousin's arm and hurry off down the corridor before quickly turning to the left and out of sight. "Come on, Indy, we need to work on another solution, and also what to do if Havers fails."

Austerley nodded and followed Kirkgordon as he raced down the corridor, Sam slung over his shoulder, opposite to his free arm, the prosthetic with the crossbow. When they had reached the corridor where Havers had turned left, they turned right. From here they ran along a short corridor and found a stairwell leading down. Carefully checking the way ahead, Kirkgordon made his way down the steps before arriving at another door. He opened it gently, scanned the corridor beyond and saw a crew door just ahead.

"We'll take that one, Indy. I guess we say goodbye to the safe room, as Sam would have known that plan. If I can get us some space, do you think we can get her back to normal? She's a damn weight and a liability to carry about."

"Maybe," said Austerley, "but I'll need the pharmacy. I could get her drugged and break the connection if they have the right things. Give her mind a shock of sorts, but there will be side effects."

"Never mind those. We'll get crew-side and see if we can't find some medical areas. It'll be further down though, medical centres are usually well below the entertainment decks."

Opening the door fully, Kirkgordon raced across to the crew door and found it locked. "Flame!" He used the fire from his bolt to burn the control pad and found the door releasing. *Thank goodness for fail safe mechanisms.* Turning to Austerley, he signalled him to follow and found himself in another corridor.

The woman had said rat, rat in a trap. That's what we are, scurrying here and there from the catcher. If we can get Sam lucid this will be a lot easier. I'm fed up carrying my team.

At the end of the new corridor, Kirkgordon found a deck plan and saw the route to the medical centre. "Just down the next set of steps for about eight decks, Indy. I guess the area might be a bit more deserted than the upper decks. I certainly hope so."

Cautiously, he made his way to the new stairwell and was glad to find it empty. As he descended, he heard noises from the corridors attached to it. As they passed the windows on the doors to those corridors, Kirkgordon kept everyone low down and clear of any onlookers. But his legs were sore, carrying someone was hard enough but crouching and carrying at the same time was causing his muscles to scream at him.

"Indy, if this woman can see through the zombies, can she use them all at once or would it be through one?"

"I don't know," said Austerley. "It's likely to be only one on a focused sense, like talking through them but she'll probably be in contact with them all, capable of sending a corporate message. If they see us, they will report back. I don't think it's something we can block. I'll have to use some pretty strong stuff with Sam and it'll…"

"Okay, I don't need details."

"But it'll…"

"Indy, hush. I need to concentrate on what I'm doing. Good, this is the deck."

Glancing through the window, Kirkgordon instantly ducked down again as a shadow passed the window. Giving himself a few seconds, he them glanced back up again and saw a zombie walking away from the door. He placed a finger on his lips and motioned Austerley through the door. With his eyes on the zombie, Kirkgordon walked backwards towards the medical centre until the zombie had turned a corner at the far end of the corridor.

"This is it," whispered Austerley. He went to open the door, but Kirkgordon slapped his hand.

"It's an open area, I'll check it first. Here, take Sam."

Austerley reluctantly dropped his shoulder and then almost toppled over when Sam was off loaded to him. *I always forget how out of shape he is, he must be knackered.*

Kirkgordon gingerly opened the medical centre door, which was transparent, and the reception area appeared to be clear. However, large amounts of papers were scattered across the floor and a printer was upturned with half of its contents hanging out. Listening intently, Kirkgordon could only hear Austerley panting outside the door. There were two doors inside the reception room, one with a toilet sign on the door, and another stating consulting room.

Kirkgordon gently tapped the toilet room door. No sound was returned. He opened the door quickly, primed to respond to an attack but was taken aback by the sight before him. A man was laid prone with a mass of blood running from his neck. Kirkgordon ignored the image for now and turned back to the consulting room door. Again he gave a gentle tap. Again nothing was returned. Quickly, he opened the door and saw a short corridor with two doors leading off it. One had a large window beside it with curtains pulled across.

Kirkgordon chose the room with the window and again tapped the door. He had determined that any zombie would race to the door and hit it full on. But he was aware that any non-zombies would have an advantage over him. He opened the door and saw a medical bed and cabinets. The bed hadn't been used recently and the surfaces were clear. A further door was at the rear of the room, possibly a washroom. Keeping up his methodology, Kirkgordon tapped and then checked inside the washroom. All was silent and undisturbed. Coming back out of the room, he heard a sound from the reception area. Quickly, he glided to the open door and saw Austerley staggering around the reception area before dumping Sam in a corner out of sight.

"Sorry, can't hold her any longer."

"Shush. Just stay low in the corner. There's a vampire victim in the toilet. You might need to make sure he's not going to come to life."

"Become one of the undead. They are not alive, a common misconception among amateurs and…"

"Shush, it's not clear yet."

Kirkgordon turned back to the consulting room door that remained unexplored. A tap on the door. Nothing in return. He swung the door open and found an unlit room. There was a medical bed in the middle of the room with equipment surrounding it. Unlike the rest of the ship so far there wasn't even an emergency light on. The hairs on Kirkgordon's neck stood up. Everywhere else there had been lights. But here there were none. He looked for the switch. It was beside the door.

Kirkgordon held his ground but let his crossbow emerge from his arm. Someone was here, something wasn't right. At the far side of the room he saw a half open cabinet door. Lowering his gaze, he was able to see under the medical bed and there was a dark fluid pooled near the cabinet. Gently creeping across the room and scanning as he did, Kirkgordon reached the pooled fluid and dipped two fingers into it. He smelt it, then rubbed it thin. Blood.

He scanned the room again. Shadow in the far corner. Now that's a lampstand. Across from it. Medical equipment. To the side of it. That's an arm. He shot a bolt straight into it. A body fell forward. A hand grabbed him by the neck and Kirkgordon was flung across the room bouncing off the bed, and dropping onto the hard floor.

He rolled as best he could and found himself being kicked. Arms flung across his face took the brunt of the blow but he was stunned, and didn't see the hand that grabbed him again and sent him into a cabinet. Kirkgordon was grabbed by the throat and lifted high. Through the darkness he saw a face with eyes of hate, a dark fury that spoke of evil.

"On your own? Always tastier when the blood is one of God's own."

16

Horrors for Hannah

Havers turned the corner with Hannah in tow and immediately started looking for somewhere he could hole up. The likelihood was that Kirkgordon and Austerley would get spotted and the heat would be taken off Hannah and himself for a little while. Kirkgordon was good, and he had courage but he hadn't been trained like Havers. It was not a great idea having Hannah along in terms of her safety, but she had knowledge that would be useful. But family never mixed well with business.

Anyway, he would need to get to this Dr Howard. By all means dispose of his lackey—this woman causing the zombification—but the link he had followed in his pursuit of Farthington was tenuous. He needed to speak to the doctor directly and find out where his contact with Farthington was coming from.

Havers saw a stairwell and headed straight into it. Coming up the stairs was a zombie, a portly gentleman who flared his teeth and tried to run hard up the stairs at Havers. But the entranced man stumbled and Havers caught him a kick to the side of the head that would knock him out cold. The turned people were fast, hungry for a fight, but they were not that agile. This was good. He didn't intend on killing any of these poor blighters who had been turned, but when needs must, he wouldn't hesitate.

Continuing up the stairwell, Havers briefly asked Hannah where the least occupied area would be. The water skiing device, "The Big Wave", on the top deck to the aft of the vessel. Nodding his approval, Havers skipped up the stairs, urging his cousin on behind him. A woman with a rabid face turned at him as he climbed. She was young, maybe late twenties, and he hit her with his shoulder, then threw her backward, cracking her head off the interior wall. Her face went silent and he skipped past ignoring the cry of Hannah, shocked at the sight.

Soon he had reached the end of the stairwell. Havers was sweating, sucking in air, but he was feeling fine. The waiter's outfit was a little restrictive but it would have to do. At the top of the stairwell, he looked through the window for potential threats. In his mind the vampires were the greatest threat, but he couldn't dismiss the zombies. They were such a mix of overweight tourists and trim sun seekers, people from a wide variety of jobs and professions. Some were bound to be more than a handful.

He also needed to be quick and decisive. Letting a zombie talk back to their mistress would give away position and the game could be up. Turning to face Hannah, he saw the little girl he used to play with, who had now grown into a professional woman, a credit to the family, and a beautiful human being.

"Are you okay, my dear?"

"Arthur, you just went straight through those people."

"Yes, but they'll live. This is not the office, dear Hannah, this is the field. I never sent you to the field."

"No," said Hannah, "It was Wilson who suggested it. He wanted the books coded, something that couldn't be broken without the code, a code that he said you'd never crack. And probably Austerley wouldn't either."

"So you are the key card, in modern parlance. He underestimates Mr Austerley. The man's mind is a whirr of mythology and madness, but he's also so far out the side of madness, he can handle the chaos that life is built on. He can make the numbers work. That is why he is so dangerous."

"Arthur, do we get out of this?"

"Of course we do."

Hannah looked at him, her eyes welling up. "Where did you go? We were worried sick. There was no word, nothing. When they said you had…, gone off that platform into…, well who knows where. Where have you been?"

"On the trail, Hannah, but now is not the time. We are not secure."

Havers opened the door and waved Hannah through behind him. Carefully, he walked along the edge of what was labelled as a running track. The night was cool, but it was also eerily quiet except for the gentle crashing of the vessel through the ocean below.

Looking at the stars, Havers wondered. *Had the vessel been turned off course?* He could not be sure, but Austerley would know. *He practically carries star charts in his head. But if we are off course then maybe the doctor is heading towards Farthington. It may be best to let this run a little. It would put everyone at risk but it would be worth it to have that dragon's head on a plate.*

The deck was lit by lights every twenty metres or so along

the wall, and it gave a false sense of being able to see. Yes, you could make out the large objects well but finer detail required one to be closer. Havers saw a large shape ahead and pulled Hannah into an alcove. A lurching man in a gym outfit wandered past, oblivious to their presence.

And then ahead Havers saw a strapping man, dressed in what seemed to be gothic clothing. In front of him was another shape, a woman from the curves she had. Plump but with large, voluminous hair. And her neck was sat at an angle. Havers quietly lead Hannah into a dark patch at the nearest wall. Holding a finger to his lips, he made sure she understood to stay there.

Creeping ever closer, he saw the vampire pick the woman up by the neck and reach with his mouth to her. The neck was already sideways, she was gone. Evidently Hannah saw it too, as she let out a muffled scream. *Move Arthur, move!*

Havers exploded towards the vampire, hitting him with his shoulder and taking him over to the barrier of the deck. Without hesitation, he grabbed the vampire's feet and lifted them up. The creature pushed out both arms, desperately trying to hold onto the barrier. Havers let go with one hand and battered the creature with his fist, knowing that he had to keep it from coming to its senses, effectively keeping it from morphing. But then a hand reached out and grabbed him.

His throat felt like it was clamped by a vice. Already breathing was difficult and this gamble of moving the vampire quickly over the side of the vessel was seeming to backfire. *Strength, Arthur, stupid Arthur. Austerley never used strength on them. Not that sort of strength. Hannah? Hannah would have one.*

His cousin had always been more into the Church of England than he ever had. His parents had never been around that much so he had only gone when his Auntie had made him. But Hannah was steeped in it. In fact, she rarely missed. And for her confirmation, she'd been given the necklace from his father. The thin chain with the little cross. Not long before he had passed on.

"Hannah," wheezed Havers. "Come here, show him your neck."

There was a squeal from Hannah. *Damn, that might bring more.* But Havers could hear her running to him. A faint shadow fell, and he knew she was close. But the air was going, he was drawing on deep resources now. He had only a few words left.

"Touch him… touch him with it."

Havers didn't see what Hannah was doing but it made the vampire start. Without hesitation, Havers ripped the hand from his throat. He saw Hannah holding the tiny cross on the chain and grabbed her hand driving it into the vampire's forehead. The vampire's flesh burned, and Hannah opened her mouth, wide in terror but no sound came from the petrified woman.

The vampire convulsed, and Havers pushed Hannah back before reaching down and driving the creature's legs up into the air, see-sawing its body over the barrier. It tumbled down, far into the depths. Havers grabbed the woman lying on the floor, and after briefly confirming she had no pulse and that her neck was broken, he hurled her over the side too. Hannah stood watching, like she had become entranced.

Havers took her hand. "We need to go. Don't think. Do!"

With great haste, Havers continued down the running track, scanning ahead whilst listening intently for any other night walker on the deck. Ahead he could see the large construction of "The Big Wave" and saw the barrier across the entrance. *Perfect, the zombies could not get past such a basic obstruction.* He thought of them like lost Alzheimer's patients, stuck at the most obvious of blockages, a hedge or a gate, with no understanding of how to move them.

He could feel Hannah shaking in his grasp. He needed to hurry. Quickly, he got her over the gate of the ride and together they ran down the entrance and then over to the operating hut. It was dark in the night sky but come dawn this place would be perfect. No zombie could reach it and no vampire could exist in the daylight. And dawn was so close now.

Once inside the little pod, he saw Hannah crumple to the floor. He sat down beside his cousin who had her open hand before her, weeping as she looked at the cross in her palm. There was blood on it, a little flesh too. And Hannah's tears were falling onto her hand, mingling there with the blood which then ran diluted across her hand.

"Shush, dearest, shush. I know. I know," whispered Havers. And he thought of his own mother and how he sat with her after her execution. The blood of her wounds had been on his hands as he held her. His first true horror. Not much got through his professional exterior, but Hannah was smashing that wall apart.

17

Name That Herb

The creature before him was a gothic nightmare. Its lips were covered with what looked like fresh blood, probably from the man on the toilet. The eyes were strangely entrancing and Kirkgordon tried an old driving technique, looking at the man's boot covered feet rather than at his face. It kept the hypnotic stare from grabbing him, but he did feel he was working with the poorest of sight, everything on the periphery.

"No Professor?" The voice was smug. "And no cross. Sloppy not carrying a cross. The Professor wouldn't make that mistake.

Kirkgordon looked around the medical room, desperate for an idea. *Stake through the heart, that's what they said, wasn't it? But this was a medical room, there's no wood in here. Maybe in the lobby. Yes, there was a wooden chair, certainly the legs. If I could break that off and use it.*

As if he was understanding Kirkgordon's train of thought the vampire edged slightly covering the door and exit to the lobby. *Damn.* Kirkgordon allowed his crossbow to emerge from his arm, and then groggily stood up with a bolt aimed at the vampire.

"I don't believe you can hurt me with that. Did the Professor tell you nothing, did he not explain to his poor student?"

"Student?" Kirkgordon was indignant. "I'm no lackey to that clown. You're looking at the boss here, plain and simple. He has nothing beyond his knowledge, he doesn't tell anyone what to do and he's practically under lock and ley. Yet you guys, you freaks seem to revere him. What is it with the undead? Other lands, fish-headed men, dragons, you all are so damn obsessed. Even Farthington was practically drooling talking to him."

The vampire started. "Farthington, how do you know Farthington?"

"No! No way. He can't be here as well. Do you realise I was going to take it easy on this one. This mission should have been about sun and Jacuzzis. I haven't even been in the pool."

"Silence, mortal. What do you know of the Farthington creature? He secured passage for us on this crazy ship. We were meant to be undisturbed. And yet, we are bothered by this ridiculous excuse of a mutiny. Humans, here and there, everywhere. None with a bit of fight in them. Dull, slow witted. Until you. What do you know about Farthington?"

Kirkgordon could see a hand coming around the open door to the corridor. It was large and slightly chubby. Austerley must have heard the commotion and come in. Well, at least he hadn't run. But what would he do? Kirkgordon needed to second guess him. In truth, they rarely worked a plan together, more just did their own thing and hoped for the best. But at least he now had an expert on scene.

"Farthington? What do you know of Farthington? Tell or I

will feast on you now."

"You'll feast on me anyway." Austerley's head had appeared around the door. *He's looking at the jars on the far wall. The herbal section.*

"But I'll feast slower if you don't tell me. Time to let me know or do you want your soul dammed to an eternal hell on this earth? Where is that wretched dragon?"

Austerley had tiptoed across to the herbal cabinet where he was picking up a jar. There then followed a strange set of signals in which his left hand seemed to imitate a bowling action, he then tapped his arm and projected something from it.

"Someone else is here. I smell the blood, Professor. I thought you would have covered your trail better than that. You have a distinct odour, and I smell fear. It is also good to have a victim that understands just what a bite can mean."

The vampire never turned to Austerley, keeping his eyes on Kirkgordon. He never saw the glass jar being lobbed in the general vicinity of the vampire but over its head. As it reached its apex, Kirkgordon fired a bolt shattering it, glass exploding and the contents, a strange substance looking like a cross between a fungi and tree bark, fell on the vampire.

"Argh! No, what is it? Burns!"

Kirkgordon didn't wait to see the effect but instead leapt at the vampire who was waving its arms at the offensive fauna that had covered him. Kirkgordon caught some in his hand and dove at the vampire's eyes with it. The creature ducked his advance and rose with an intention to sink its teeth into Kirkgordon's shoulder. Seeing the attack, Kirkgordon flung his crossbow arm across and the vampire got a mouthful of prosthetic hand and arm.

"Cover him in the Aconitum."

"What? What the hell's that, Indy?"

"The contents of the jar."

Kirkgordon was now attached to the vampire by the arm and couldn't pull away from its mouth. He felt a massive blow to his stomach and realised just how strong the creature was. With his free arm, he flailed for a piece of whatever Austerley had thrown but found none. It was then that he saw the hulking figure of the Professor above him. Austerley grabbed some of the substance and drove it into the creature's eyes.

"Aconitum! Wolfsbane, Churchy. It's wolfsbane, they can't take it. Herbal medicine, cures so much."

The creature thrashed and threw off Kirkgordon but managed to lay a hand on Austerley. But it had grabbed his leg from its prone position and sunk its teeth into the Professor's ankle.

"Jam it in, Austerley. Keep its mouth full, then it can't bite."

Although not a fighter, Austerley was a hulk of a man and drove all the weight he had behind his foot, deep into the vampire's mouth.

"Get a bucket or something, and fill it with water," cried Austerley. "And bless it. Bless the damn water."

Kirkgordon scanned around quickly. There was a small stainless steel bowl on the side and he grabbed it, throwing it under the tap. "So just like last time? I don't need to have my hand in it because it's water, do I?"

"No, just do it! Just say a prayer over it, ask God into it, something like that. Do it now, my foots detaching!"

Kirkgordon mumbled a prayer over the water, something about needing a little help and sorry for all the lack of talking. And then he just begged, give me this. He heard Austerley fall over and saw him on the ground, footless, and desperately rolling away from the now rising vampire. Kirkgordon threw the bowl and contents right at his head.

There was a cry of pain and the skin of the vampire seemed to burn away like it had been consumed with acid. And Kirkgordon saw in its eyes, the horror of death as it knew its time was up.

"To hell with you. They'll unleash the brood to look for you." The vampire fell to the ground and became still as half its face dissolved. There was no blood or any other fluids or internals you would expect from a human in that situation. Kirkgordon realised that they truly were dead on the inside.

"Dammit, we can't take too many of them. If I knew there were going to be vampires I'd have prepped up. This makeshift bollocks is not going to hold out for us."

Kirkgordon lifted a soaked prosthetic foot from what remained of the vampire and handed it to the prone Austerley.

"Here, Indy. Wolfsbane? What the hell was in that jar?"

"There's a small range of Chinese herbal medicine there and that jar contains Aconitum. Also known as wolfsbane, monkswood, mousebane, devils helmet. Whatever they call it, it's more lethal than garlic to a vampire. You did well because he was a strong one. But your vampire knowledge is plain bollocks."

"Thanks, Indy. I'll make it my goal to know the undead better in the future."

After assisting Austerley to put his foot back into its socket, Kirkgordon quickly scouted the corridor to see if anyone was about. When he found no one, he blocked the door with the reception table and took Sam into the little single bed side ward and laid her down.

"If we lock this door and tie her to the bed, maybe she'll come to no harm until we sort this out," said Kirkgordon.

Austerley reached past him and opened Sam's eyes. He was holding a small torch from the consulting room and shone it into her eyes. They didn't move but the pupils contracted.

"That's interesting. There's body function in there. It's not full control, just suggestibility. Like I said before, they ain't zombies like a virus has attacked them, one of those movie plot types. No, this is control, hypnotic of a sort. I think I should try to break it. I'll check the room next door and see if we have the necessary substances to effect a break."

Austerley disappeared into the room, and Kirkgordon was left alone with Sam. Her hair, long and blonde, was splayed across the pillow—she seemed so peaceful. But the playful life that he had known briefly of her was also gone. She gave him a strange feeling, like he was looking at a shell, a beautiful shell, but the essence was gone. But thankfully there wasn't anyone else looking out at him from inside either. *How do I get in a situation to think about these problems? Woman trouble takes on a whole new meaning around Austerley.*

It was twenty minutes before Austerley returned, and he had a solution in a small phial as well as a needle.

"Are you sure about this?" asked Kirkgordon.

"Not overly. I also haven't got a lot of solution here either, so it's not a cure I can offer to others. You should also note, she may be a bit exuberant when she awakes. And not totally functioning. Well, a bit open, I'd say. Honest."

"Okay, whatever, but there's no serious side effects?"

"Every side effect can be serious."

"But nothing to harm her."

"Well…, no."

"Then do it." Kirkgordon watched Austerley slide the needle into Sam's arm and saw her body contort briefly before she lay silent again but with a smile on her face.

"That's good," said Austerley. "But we need to wake her to make it take full effect."

"Okay. Sam, Sam, wake up. Come on." He tapped her arm and then her face gently. Sam murmured something, her eyes beginning to open, and she seemed extremely happy. As her eyes opened more fully and she apparently began to focus, Kirkgordon thought she began to recognise him.

"Oh, so good, so good. Those hands are…, so good." She looked at the bed around her. "It'll do." Sam reached up and hauled Kirkgordon's face to hers, devouring his mouth with her own. Breaking off briefly, she moaned before announcing, "Show me what a secret agent can do!"

18

Havers On Deck

Hannah had fallen asleep and Havers thought it best to wait until the dawn was more fully established before rousing her. The sun was producing such a pure and brilliant light that Havers felt almost blind every time he glanced out of the "Big Wave" hut's window. As he sat, he realised the vessel was on a different course to what was intended. The sun was rising in a different quarter than it should. His idea of their true course was rough, but it was into the middle of the Bermuda Triangle.

At least above deck there would be no vampires. He had always hated the undead, it was like unfinished business. Wraiths, vampires, ghosts, all just hanging about taking up space on this or another world, when they had already had their time. And the issue with vampires was that they were unbelievably strong. And clever. One or other was fine, but not both together.

He knew he should take the cross from Hannah as he was easily the better fighter and a better exponent of quick thinking and vampire destruction. But in her hands, it was more potent. In her hands it could burn on touch. It could suck the soul.., that wasn't right, but it could make them become properly dead. Eradicate them. He chewed over the word. It didn't do the process justice.

Fortunately, the operators of the "Big Wave" had found it necessary to have refreshment whilst on duty and a small stack of water bottles were found just inside the door. Some crisps and chocolate bars were also there. It messed up his dedicated diet that he had adhered to as best he could for the last twenty years, a diet that had kept him in shape with regards to both mind and body, but food was food.

Hannah had found it hard to eat but he had made her. Who knew when the next meal would be? As she lay in his arms, he remembered the cousin who was always in her books, always studying, but who also shared his love of the mythologies of the world. She had been obsessed with Icarus and how to build a set of wings when she was just seven. Luckily, her father had stopped her from launching herself off the family greenhouse with an exo-skeleton of branches and leaves. Although to this day, Havers had found her attention to detail remarkable, to such a degree, he believed that she may not have flown but she would probably have at least glided.

"You're coming to, my dear. It's okay. Sun's up. No vampires and the gates will stop the zombies. You can enjoy your water and crisps in peace."

"What flavour?" asked Hannah.

"Ready salted. You never liked plain crisps."

"No, but I guess a full English is out of the question."

"Shortly we'll have breakfast at the Ritz, all the trimmings, my dear. Sort of thing your mother would have enjoyed. She always liked things done properly. The china cups. Very wise woman too. You cannot underestimate the importance of doing things well."

"Arthur? How do we do this well? What's the plan? Before we were getting safe but now we need to work this out. How are you going to get close to the Doctor? We have no weapons."

"No, we don't, but they must arm themselves on the vessel, surely. Do you know where they would keep the firearms? Although I'm thinking they wouldn't be allowed to carry any, if they docked at a civilian port. I chose not to carry whilst acting as a waiter. But then I didn't foresee this craziness."

"There's no guns. But I believe they do archery on board," advised Hannah, munching her way through her crisps.

"Good. Mr Kirkgordon would have been the man for that, but it will have to be me. Besides, I see his hand and arm are no longer his own."

"The open deck sports area is on deck fifteen, close to the top. It's about half way along the ship from here and another deck up. It should be in daylight for the most part."

"I doubt we shall be troubled by the vampires this high up as I would expect them to have gone deep inside to avoid any light. But we should still be careful. I want to be on the move in about five minutes, so drink up Hannah."

After finishing their rations, Havers led Hannah out of the proportionately safe area of the "Big Wave". The water wasn't running along the curved surface that usually had surfers all over it and Havers kept the pace slow so as Hannah wouldn't make too much noise on the metallic walkways. He could see zombies roaming the deck, but knowing they were as innocent as anyone on this boat, Havers decided that avoiding any conflict was the best policy.

This time, rather than keep to the running track which

circled the deck, Havers chose to move down the small corridors that occupied the centre. Although they were enclosed to a degree, those on the edge had plenty of sunlight. There were also plenty of doors to hand should they need to duck inside away from unwanted encounters.

Havers was aware that the whole trip must be a blur to Hannah as they moved quickly and quietly along the deck. Taking her around a corner in amongst a shower block near to a central pool, he heard her stumble and turned quickly to try and catch her. But she landed hard with a clatter. Havers grabbed her and pulled her into an open cubicle. Her chin was bleeding and he ripped a piece of his shirt off and gave it to her, advising her to apply pressure.

A hand pulled him backwards and he was thrown into the wall of the cubicle. *Guard was down for Hannah. Stupid.* There was a blur of fists coming at him which he only just got his arms in the way of. *Coloured attacker. Tall, six foot. Fast.* He was thrown again into the wall but managed to take the blow on the shoulder and roll off the wall into a fighting stance.

The attacker again moved quickly and rained successive blows down, but Havers was now prepared and after blocking a few, waited for the longer lunge that threw his opponent slightly off balance before grabbing the arm and then dropping to the floor and sweeping his leg around, tipping the attacker up. As they landed on their back, Havers jumped on top and quickly wrapped his legs around theirs whilst locking his arm around their neck. Slowly, but with maximum pressure he constricted their neck.

"You're no zombie," he said quietly and without panic. He heard Hannah weeping. "Hannah, shush, we can't be interrupted when I'm like this."

The attacker was clothed in shorts and a t-shirt but had a figure that boasted muscle. From his viewing point beside the attacker's face he realised that he was dealing with a man, the shaved face apparent. And not one that chose a superior blade with which to preen his face. If there was one thing Havers pitied in a man, it was poor personal grooming.

"Who are you?" The man refused to answer and Havers kept the choke hold on him. "Again, who are you?"

"Is he one of the Doctor's people?" asked Hannah, still clutching the piece of clothing to her chin.

"I don't know. I haven't met all of them, in fact, I've barely met any of them."

"There's a mark on his arm," Hannah observed. "It's definitely something. Looks like a hand holding seaweed, lifting it out of water. I've never seen it before. But Kirkgordon said Austerley had saved someone with a similar marking. I never asked what, though. You would have, Arthur, you're good on the small details."

The man started to tap Havers' arm. Taking it as a sign of submission, Havers released his choke slightly, barely enough to speak.

"Speak now, or I will choke you to sleep."

"My…, my name…, is Cairo. And…, you are…, on a vessel…, with the…, attention…, that how you say?"

"Intention," corrected Havers, "Go on, you have my attention."

"Yes…intention to sail…to Vil la anba vag yo…you say…Atlantis maybe…but it…is not…it is…"

"The city beneath the waves," interrupted Hannah.

"Not the other Atlantis."

"But that was only a rumour," said Hannah.

121

"It is no…rumour…we protect…I was here…with…Alexandria…but she was…attacked…and saved by…large man."

"The woman Austerley was talking about."

Havers nodded. "Why do you need to stop them? What is there?"

"For years…we have stopped the call…stopped the surface dwellers…killed them…lost ships…flying boats too."

"You have been using the Triangle to disguise this? But why? What does the city hold? Surely they are all dead?"

"People dead…but some…things…somethings…they do not die… Madichon an nan dlo a."

There was a crunch inside the man's mouth and he started to foam. Havers released him but recognised the smell of the poison coming from an internal capsule. He stood up and watched the man writhe on the ground briefly before his death. Hannah simply turned away.

"He's gone now. The worst of it is done," announced Havers.

"He said, the curse of the water, the city beneath the waves and they are all dead but there's still the curse of the water. Arthur, do you know what that means?"

"No. I'd heard of the city, not Atlantis but a separate city, unknown where, capable of travelling under the sea. And it would surface. But I am unaware of this curse," advised Havers, "Do you know of it?"

"When we visited Haiti, when we were young and could speak creole, unlike the rest of the family, do you remember?" Havers nodded. "Well, because I could speak to the elder in the tribe, he would converse with me. My parents saw it as a good language practice, but he told me tales that intrigued, myths and stories. He told one about the destruction of the city that appeared from the sea.

"It was a tale that began with two warring houses in the city, looking to seize control. The weaker was thought to lose all control and its head called out to a power from beyond, maybe Elder in origin. The name as I recall had an edge to it, like Cthulhu or Nyarlathotep. But it was a being from the deep. Maybe earthly recesses or maybe a portal. But it was dark and without a soul, the tribal elder said.

"When they made the deal, they promised the city to the Elder being but when they took over, they broke that contract. And the being took it down to the deep."

"But what's the curse of the water?" asked Havers, "I mean, let the city lie, why dig it up?"

"Because the power they were given is still there. The tribal elder said it could be harnessed but eventually the curse would unseat the user. And all related to it."

"When you say related, you don't mean by blood."

"No, he said the curse took all the subsea dwellers of the city and killed them all. He warned me that if a hand from the surface ever took that power, it would mean a destruction of the earth."

"And what does this power look like?"

"I don't know, Arthur, I really don't know or understand. But the Haitians never spoke about it, except in their own language."

"If this is all correct then we need to put these people down, Hannah. We need to call for the backup and simply stop this vessel moving. Do you have a transponder? The emergency switch?"

"It's been pressed but I'm seeing nil response."

"Then it's a damn good show that I'm here. Farthington will have to wait."

19

Someone's Enticed!

"What the heck is up with her, Indy?" asked Kirkgordon, "She's all over me."

"I didn't think that would bother you. I mean, you were flirting with her anyway."

"This isn't flirting, she's practically jumping me."

"Never seen you complain about that before. When Calandra was all over you, you didn't fight her off."

"Stop. Don't go there. That is different."

"Of course. She's a brunette."

"Indy!"

"It's the nature of the chemicals, it snaps her away from control by driving her towards her inner longings. Everything she's saying is just what she'd say without normal conventions in place. Quite refreshing really."

"And not required right now. We can't really stay here, can we?"

Austerley shook his head. "We have fresh blood, so that's going to attract our undead guests. And then there's the zombies roaming. We are kind of cornered here."

"That's my main worry. Will they start a systematic search with the zombies? Can they do that?"

"It's certainly possible, seeing how far entranced Sam was. That woman who sent the disturbance in the water that I countered, she was powerful. It wasn't a little parlour trick. And controlling this number of people is no mean feat. Of course I doubt everyone is a zombie. With the requirement to drink the free beverage and the need to see the signs some people must have been bypassed. Whether they are still alive, though, I don't know."

Kirkgordon sat down on a medical stool and Sam's arms quickly wrapped around his neck.

"They have scrubs in here. People say I look good in scrubs, it's the curves you see. They say I have good curves. I can show you in the…"

"Sam, not now, not here. We have a situation. People could be dying up there."

"But we're safe. But where's Hannah, that girl he fancies." Sam was pointing at Austerley.

"I think you are mistaken," countered Austerley.

"No, he definitely fancies her. He was constantly looking at her bum, dropping behind her when walking like you guys do."

"Sam!" warned Kirkgordon, "We need to work here. Whoever likes whoever isn't that important at the moment. Okay? That needs to wait."

"Well, I don't want to wait. I could go with you and…"

"Sam!" warned Kirkgordon. *I am the master of bad timing. My wife is a mess, my would-be lover has to keep miles away and then this bundle of fun appears. Another world, another time, always the same story.*

"We're still in the dark," said Austerley, "about where we are going. The vessel may have changed course too, but I can't tell without the stars or the sun. Or some actual instruments on the bridge, but I doubt we'll get near that."

"Yeah, but don't you find something strange about all this?" asked Kirkgordon. "Hijack a ship. It's slow, it can't get you anywhere quick, so it must be needed as what will happen is going to happen on the sea. But what is near here, apart from the Bermuda Triangle? Nothing. And there's nothing in the Triangle, I mean it's been investigated loads, yes?"

"I saw it on one of those documentary channels, something is in the water. They said Atlantis was here," ventured Sam.

"That's misguided speculation," said Austerley. "Atlantis is off south west Morocco and is deep down. But there are other islands that sink. Although there's been none of those in this region that I can recall."

"Oh," said Sam, "And you know all of them, do you? You're not as gorgeous as my Kirky, here."

"Sam, focus," said Kirkgordon and daring Austerley to take advantage.

"Actually I am one of the world's foremost experts on such matters."

"Is he?"

Kirkgordon nodded.

"Doesn't look it. I prefer sexy experts," said Sam cuddling into Kirkgordon's back.

"Let's go up top then. See if you can work out where we are going," said Kirkgordon. "I don't think we should get in Havers' way but we can raise a little hell."

"I'd raise hell with…"

"Sam!"

Austerley quickly scoured the medical room looking for any items that might be of use and pocketed two jars and also grabbed two bottles of water. These he handed to Kirkgordon, insisting he bless them. Fighting off Sam's attempts to have Kirkgordon bless her, Kirkgordon did as asked and then grabbed a few energy bars he found by the bedside in the room adjacent to the consulting room.

With everything prepared, Kirkgordon took a hold of Austerley's arm.

"Is there anything else I should be aware of with regard to Sam?"

"Well, she is likely to feel a little bit more heroic, may leap to defend you. But she will also feel very little pain for a while. The *Superwoman* effect, I call it. And as she has the hots for you, our resident Sir Galahad, then you need to keep her on a leash, she's liable to take on anything for you."

"Just magic. She's a civilian, so we keep her safe, Austerley. Are sure she's totally clear of the zombie influence?"

"Oh yes. She might bed you, but she won't kill you."

"Thanks, Indy. Really well put. Thanks."

The small party moved out into the lobby of the medical suite, and Kirkgordon released the furniture he had put at the door. As he leaned out of the door, scanning the hall, he felt something pinch his ass. There wasn't time for a rebuke and try as hard as he could to just simply focus, he recognised his enjoyment of the moment, especially as he felt her leaning into him.

Life had been lonely, Alana simply wasn't the woman he had remembered, not that she was to blame. Calandra's going away and then the brief meeting on the snowy slopes of the Alps, tore at him more than he could say. And then in comes

Sam with no conditions, no agenda or weirdness. And she just wanted some fun. And she wasn't a witch like Tania. Then he remembered the days when he looked at a woman and just thought she looks nice, rather than assessing whether she was a freak or an evil being.

With the corridor clear, Kirkgordon crept along slowly, particularly wary of vampires. There was still power in the vessel which was comforting, as the people wouldn't be without power and food, if rescue took a while. That was those who were still alive, if they hadn't succumbed to a vampire or a zombie fight. *Anyway, focus on the job in hand. Surface and quickly.*

Kirkgordon realised he was distracted with his thoughts as a door opened beside him and a portly gentleman stepped between him and Sam. Before he could react, Sam hit the man with a punch to the chin and Kirkgordon watched him fall to the floor. As he fell back into the cabin, they heard a woman cry out. Kirkgordon dove through the door and saw an elderly woman, her face almost white with fright.

"Austerley, get everyone in here," Kirkgordon said in a harsh whisper as he grabbed the elderly woman and clasped a hand across her mouth. With great moaning, Austerley dragged the man inside the cabin and shut the door once Sam had also bounded inside, smiling at her efforts.

"He was going to have you," said Sam and flung her arms around Kirkgordon.

"No, Sam, he wasn't. Austerley, is he okay?"

"Well," said Austerley, examining the man carefully, "he's out cold but otherwise, yes, I think he's going to be okay."

"Thank God. Sam, you need to wait before you hit someone." Kirkgordon could feel the elderly woman trembling. "Sam,

128

make this woman a cup of tea."

Sam beamed at him and instantly sought the kettle. Taking the elderly woman's hand, he led her to a chair and sat her down but kept his hand on her mouth.

"Listen, we mean you no harm. This was an accident but you are in grave danger. I will need you to lock the door after we go and then stay in here. Don't open the door." The woman had a blank look on her face. "Comprendez-vous?" He released the hand.

"Warten Sie auf mich damit Sie mich töten können?"

"It's German, Churchy, and no she doesn't. I'll deal with it."

"Okay, but no explanations to scare her. Just the basics, stay inside and bar the door. And invite no one in."

There's no balcony here. Just a single room, locked in. Unless they make ridiculous noises or open the door, they should be safe enough. She's too old to take with us. He watched Austerley talk with her and was actually impressed. The old woman seemed to take to him and when her son, as it turned out, awoke, she was able to diffuse his worries and surprise. Sam, however, was still beaming at Kirkgordon. This wasn't going away quickly.

The small party left the cabin and made their way towards a stairwell that lead up to the open decks at the top of the ship. Kirkgordon lead and had to step over several bodies on the way up. One of them had its neck torn out, and Austerley checked to see if the body would rise again as an undead. But it was not so, and Kirkgordon told the party to continue, feeling wrong about not doing something to give the person some dignity.

The climb up the stairwell was a long one as they moved slowly, but caution was essential as several times they had to creep past corridors where zombies roamed. Keeping quiet was critical to staying alive, and for all her exuberance, Sam seemed to follow this direction.

As they reached the last door of the stairwell, which Kirkgordon reckoned was about 3 decks from the very top but was an open deck, he spotted a small party on the move. There was the woman with whom Austerley had tangled and Dr Howard. They were surrounded by zombies and several henchmen of the large built variety.

"Austerley, he's on deck."

"Who?"

"Howard, he's got binoculars and is looking for something. We must be close to the place. Whatever the place is?"

"Can you see anything on the water?"

"No. I can get a shot at him though. It's a long one but I could try and take him out. Better though if you two moved and I did it without you here, in case it doesn't work."

"I could try something," said Austerley, "but as soon as I do she'll know where we are. If it doesn't work then…"

"We'll be for it." Sam had crawled up beside Kirkgordon and was looking through the window. "But he needs taken out, we could end this right here," said Kirkgordon

"Is that Dr Howard, the man you want stopped?" asked Sam.

"Yes, Sam," said Kirkgordon and turned to Austerley to discuss things further. But the door of the stairwell opened and Sam started running towards the party looking out to sea. She was waving her arms and crying obscenities at Dr Howard.

Kirkgordon gulped. "Shit!"

20

Infiltration

H avers sat on his backside with his shoulders pinned to the white wall. Hannah was pinned tight beside him, and he had to juke his head around the corner to see part of the bridge. The bridge itself was as immense as any he had ever seen, and he wondered if there were too many people about to make a devastating entrance. It was one thing to have the element of surprise, quite another if you had to put down forty people before you could take advantage of that surprise.

He briefly looked at his companion. The girl was holding up well, but then she always had whenever they were younger and were playing, running along dodgy edges, spying on her parents. The day they had caught her father in the bedroom with a maid was particularly rough on Hannah but she had managed to contain her emotions. A month later her mother had found out and slung her father a right hook Kirkgordon would have been proud of. They had stayed together, but the relationship was seemingly never the same.

He needed to get inside the bridge and see where they

were and what the intentions were. Also to understand how forces were deployed so he could effect a containment on any of Dr Howard's men. Moving about like that would be easier if Hannah wasn't with him. Looking around, he saw a housing which seemed to contain some vents and was almost a man high. Pointing to Hannah, he crept towards it with her following.

Quickly, and with a deftness of touch, Havers closed the doors of the large vent and brought Hannah's ear close to his so he could whisper to her.

"I need to get close and see what is what on the bridge. We'll never create a mutiny on our own. Also, if Dr Howard is there, I'll have a better chance of assassination on my own. Thank you for your help, it has been extremely useful. If I'm not back in an hour, go back down and hole up somewhere. Interior cabin might be best. Act like you don't know anything or be a zombie. Just stay safe, Hannah."

"You too, Arthur. The family wants you back, you know that. Your family, my family, or what's left of it."

Havers nodded and without hesitating opened the doors of the vent and left, closing them gently behind him. Hannah would be alright. She'd have to be.

The best way to move about the bridge was, of course, to get a disguise but then again how big a crew did Howard have? *If he's got a tight crew then I'll be an obvious stranger,* thought Havers. *But if he's searching for something important, he might have a load of disposables who are just jumping to the tune. It's worth the risk.*

Finding a door to the internal side of the bridge, Havers moved with a grace that defied his masculine demeanour. Although wiry, he was still strongly built but benefitted from the ballet lessons he had been taught at a young age. His mother and father had always prepared him for this life, even though he lost them at a relatively young age.

The corridor he entered was narrow and ran towards and away from the bridge. There were pipes running up the side of the corridor and covered electrical cables, tastefully designed so as not to stand out but available for easy access. Havers had never been a mariner, but he recognised good workmanship. This truly was one of the classiest vessels he had ever known.

From behind him he heard someone in the corridor, and he dropped into a small alcove. As the man walked past, Havers simply reached out and pulled him in, the neck being broken almost instantly. The man was wearing a black jumpsuit with an assortment of weapons and a bullet proof vest. *Good, it's a goon.* Knowing he was vulnerable, Havers stripped the man and changed into his clothing. It was a little large, but it would do. The weapons would be particularly helpful. There was a small handgun, a semi-automatic and some flashbangs and grenades of sorts. Obviously the Doctor had expected possible resistance from the authorities. *Well, it certainly would not go amiss.*

Leaving the man momentarily propped up into the alcove, Havers quickly went in the opposite direction from the bridge until he found what looked like a metal box with a lid in a second alcove. Opening the lid, he found it empty. It had possibly been a flare store, ropes, charts, documents, who knew, not him. Regardless, it would make a good morgue.

Retreating quickly up the corridor, Havers dragged the body of the man he had killed back to the box and pushed the figure into the small space. He had to fold him, at times cracking bones. With a detachment suitable for a long term operative,

Havers shut the lid of the box without a word, focused on his next task.

With his weapon shouldered, he walked along the corridor to the bridge where he heard voices. There seemed to be an argument going on, and Havers stopped short of the main bridge door.

"This is where it should be. Dr Howard employed me to get this vessel into the right place, and it is here. We shall be switching off engines and drifting within twenty minutes and that will have us at a safe distance from the latitude and longitude he provided. If he wants to get closer once it has surfaced, then by all means, but I recommend not going too close until it surfaces."

The other side of the conversation was quieter and Havers struggled to hear. But then the new master of the vessel spoke again.

"If she wants, then of course…whatever she asks."

There was a sound from behind him and Havers realised that someone was coming behind him. Standing upright, he brought himself to an imposing bearing and opened the door onto the bridge. Without a moment's hesitation, he walked right into the ship's command centre.

There was a seat in the middle of the bridge that would have afforded an amazing view of the ocean ahead. Banks of equipment sat on either side and various workstations were occupied by people who seemed to be actual crew, albeit Dr Howard's crew. There were also a few men with weapons who seemed to be standing to the side. One of them was making his way over to Havers.

"Been told there may be some trouble heading this way," said Havers. "Are we still secure up here?"

"Yes, have you been sent up from Tango?" asked the guard.

"Affirm, as backup until we have hunted down these difficulties."

"Okay, stay here, I'm going to send one of my men on a sweep around the bridge."

Havers gave a nonchalant nod and started to wander around the bridge, apparently looking out of any viewing access to the ship's deck. But his eyes were wandering across control desks, looking for the one thing he knew something about. It would be a button, stowed away safely for it would send off a beacon alert that the ship was being hijacked, or at least in difficulty. It wouldn't get help here very quick, but it would get help.

Hannah had said she had activated the signal all agents carried for SETAA. He had carried one once before his search for Farthington had intensified. He wasn't even sure he would be welcome back at the agency given that he had gone rogue. But maybe someone was blocking that signal, that cry for help. But the one on the bridge would be part of the ship's function. *If I was them, I'd even set up a test to show how alright the vessel was. It's worth a shot to press it.*

But where was it? Surely it wouldn't be far from the Master, somewhere on the bridge, obvious but protected from accidental activation…and hidden from sight so it wouldn't be easily destroyed by any miscreants. Havers swung his eyes around, keeping his head in a fixed attitude to allay suspicion. *Somewhere, it's somewhere around here.* He drifted towards the main panel beside the main chair on the bridge. Then it caught his eye.

So as not to raise anyone's attention to him, he continued to walk around the bridge, looking out the window, here and there, as if he was looking for a would-be attacker.

"Send a message to the Doctor, we are now in positon as asked and will use only light thrusters to control our drift. It is only ten minutes until eruption," advised the Master.

Eruption. It's actually coming up here. Time to get a move on. Havers pretended to check around the front of the bridge looking out but then turned and walked up to the panel beside the main chair. Without hesitation, he reached to a covered button on the underside, flipped away the plastic button and pressed it hard. Not missing a moment, he then replaced the cover before walking back to the front of the bridge as if he had remembered seeing something strange.

What was the next move? I need to get to Dr Howard. If the city is going to rise, then I need to stop whoever can tap into its power. I need to get off the bridge and get to where they are going to take a landing party across. Time to make an excuse and go.

Havers pretended to look at his watch and then went to walk from his view at the bridge window. But something was pressed into the back of his neck. He recognised the end of a handgun. Well, the button had been a risk.

"Turn around, and keep your hands up," said a voice. On turning around, Havers saw a mercenary dressed in black with a handgun now to his temple and two others flanking him with automatic guns trained on him. "You," the man said to an associate, "remove his weapons and check him carefully, the Doctor has some strange enemies, and even stranger friends."

Havers' weapons were removed except for those in his mouth. *No one ever checks in there*, he thought. *Even in Dillingham they never checked.*

"Tie his hands up and his feet and dump him at the front of the bridge. If he has any friends then they can see his brains getting blown out at the bridge window as a message to sod off."

Havers didn't resist but instead was glad to have a view as the island was going to rise. *When they are watching it, that'll be the time. Never had an island as a distraction before.*

21

Chaos on deck!

Sam was letting loose with her tongue at a bemused party who were more focused on what was happening in the sea just alongside the ship. With a dismissive hand, the woman who had been controlling the zombies sent two guards to deal with the mad woman approaching the party.

"Dammit, Austerley, she'll get herself killed. Cover me!" yelled Kirkgordon as he burst out of the door after Sam.

"Cover you?" shouted Austerley behind him, "With what?"

Ignoring the comment, Kirkgordon let his arm open up and fired off a bolt in the direction of the guards moving to intercept Sam. They seemed somewhat bemused by the sudden appearance of this new attacker.

Sam was about twenty yards ahead of Kirkgordon having stolen the initiative but he was gaining quickly. He was sure he could reach her before the guards, but he saw their automatic weapons at their side and decided that something larger was required. "Flame!" He fired a bolt ahead of Sam and watched it erupt on contact with the boat deck, causing a fire. Sam reared at the heat and Kirkgordon was with her and pulling her off to the side as he heard the bullets begin to fly. The flames had provided good cover, but it wouldn't do for long.

As he pulled Sam to the side, he saw through the flames the Doctor leaning over the edge of the vessel seemingly unperturbed by this sudden scene of confusion. He was watching intently and smiling at something beyond the boat. There was a chance. He stopped and took a knee to steady himself. Arms were flung around him, and he felt himself being kissed. *Bloody hell, not now woman.* And as he called up a bolt, he steadied as best he could despite the hands roaming across him and fired a bolt.

The Doctor reared as the bolt glanced his temple. *Damn.* And Kirkgordon was back up and running for cover. It was then he heard Austerley yelling at the guards. *What's the idiot doing?* As he cleared Sam to an alcove in the deck side, at the entrance to some toilets, he watched Austerley, whilst waving at him to get clear. Austerley was waving his hands in the fashion of a private dancer. With his size and ridiculous Hawaiian shirt, it looked like the scene from a comedy movie, but Kirkgordon knew Indy rarely did anything for show. He saw a localized disturbance of air coming from Austerley's hands and watched this move towards the fire that was burning. It blew the flames right into the guards on the other side.

Kirkgordon saw that the party that had been looking out to sea were now visibly excited, but they were also watching the developing situation on deck. The dark skinned woman beside Dr Howard started to make signs with her hands as well, and Kirkgordon looked for the danger that would come. He couldn't see anything, but Austerley seemed to be reacting.

Austerley seemed obsessed with the area around his feet. Watching in horror, Kirkgordon saw a circle cracking on the deck around his colleague who had begun tracing the line around him. As quick as the deck was cracking Austerley was forming a cold seal, an ice bond holding the deck together. More cracks developed, and Austerley kept reacting. Soon, it looked like a patchwork quilt.

There was shout from Dr Howard, and more guards made their way towards Austerley. Weapons drawn, Austerley was a sitting duck, occupied as he was with the attentions of the dark skinned woman. Kirkgordon pushed Sam behind him and opened up fire with a multitude of bolts. Down on one knee he was back to his accurate best, sending most of the guards running after he had dropped three in a matter of seconds.

And then he felt it. Something hit the vessel from underneath, causing it to tip to port severely, throwing everyone to the deck. Austerley went down hard and then the deck around him collapsed, and he fell into the hole created.

"No! Indy!" There was moment's hesitation. He couldn't leave Sam unprotected. But Austerley was down, exposed if he had survived. "Come on, Sam."

Taking Sam's hand, Kirkgordon pulled her to her feet and then took her on a run. With his free hand, he fired off bolt after bolt, deterring anyone else from getting to their feet. As he approached the hole, he saw the cracked decking and the dust cloud erupting from the hole.

"Grab hold of me, Sam," he yelled and shouted, "Rope!" His crossbow now had a bolt with a modern grappling hook attached. He swept Sam up with his arm and felt her gripping tight. Together they leapt into the hole, and Kirkgordon let his bolt fire out to the side. The hook, which was compacted, erupted into the wall around the deck, broke through and then, as the rope was pulled back by the weight on it, spikes whipped out and formed a tight grip on the wall.

Kirkgordon dropped with Sam, realising that the deck below was a lot deeper than expected. Maybe a two floor drop. But as he saw the floor rising, he let the rope tighten and together the couple began to swing and were thrown to the side as Kirkgordon sent out a thought which cut the rope. They clattered into an array of workout mats.

Kirkgordon was quickly onto his feet. He spied Austerley lying prone on the floor and raced to his side, quickly grabbing him by his jacket.

"Come on before someone looks down this hole."

Austerley was mumbling as he was dragged clear, and Kirkgordon realised that Austerley had gone into his "Mother Hydra" paralysis. Kirkgordon was astonished he had held it together during the gunfire for so long. But now he was shaking and chattering about Dagon and all manner of strange words.

Sam was standing up in the pile of mats, shaking her head and holding an elbow. She saw Kirkgordon dragging Austerley and ran over to help, but her arm gave way when she pulled at the fitting man on the floor. "What's up with him?"

"He goes like this with gunfire. It's from a time when we first met, a bad time. But he held it together there more than I've ever seen him. He's doing better. Kirkgordon saw Sam give him a look and realised that she wasn't in an emotional high anymore. "And you're fine too."

"Sorry. I don't know what…"

"It was the drugs," said Kirkgordon, still dragging Austerley clear, "and don't apologise, it wasn't your fault. In another

141

place it would have been…, yeah, really good. What do you remember?"

"Everything. Even when she spoke through me. And of course, kissing you. That was…, well, good."

Sam was actually blushing and Kirkgordon wondered just what their connection was, had it grown deeper than just a bit of fun. But there was no time and they needed to get moving. The ship was obviously aground on the island that had appeared and no doubt, Dr Howard and his people would be making their way onto the island. Havers obviously hadn't achieved his goal and who knew if he was even alive anymore?

"Sam, I believe that Dr Howard will be going onto the island that's appeared, the one that caused the ship to jolt. What he wants is there, whatever it is, so I need to trail him. You can hide up somewhere here if you want. I have to take Austerley with me, jabbering wreck that he is at the moment, because he understands this stuff. But you can hole up. It'll probably be dangerous. We may not even come back."

"You need me. How are you going to cope carrying him? At least I can help. Better to go out fighting than hiding away here. And I can always yell at them. That worked well last time."

Kirkgordon laughed and saw something in her that reminded him once again of Alana, his disturbed wife. He realised just how much he valued those prepared to stand with him, even Austerley had pierced his skin that way, insane madman that he was. He stopped dragging Austerley and took Sam's cheeks in his hands and pulled her close. He gave her a very tender kiss just on the lips. "Thank you."

Who knows how I deal with it all if we walk out of this alive. Three women, three different women, am I wise? A man's barely

142

built for one.

Reaching down, Kirkgordon hauled Austerley up and flung him onto his shoulder. *This is becoming too damn common. And I think he's put on weight.* He saw Sam point to the nearest door and he nodded. Sam opened the door, and Kirkgordon let his arm initiate with the crossbow before juking out with his head. There was a guard running down the corridor, and Kirkgordon unleashed a bolt, taking him clean off his feet.

They'll go down to where the launches go, probably. That's a heck of a way down through tight corridors and carrying Austerley. It might be easier to go up on deck and shoot a rope down. Sometimes this new arm is just fantastic.

Sam had followed him out of the door and was pointing out the stairwell along the corridor but that was the one they would be coming down from. Instead, Kirkgordon ran down the corridor and cut a path to the interior of the ship. He darted via a crisscross pattern and made for the other end of the ship where Dr Howard's party had been.

As he turned one corner, he found a zombie in his path and turned his shoulder to stop and run the other way. However, Austerley's momentum on his shoulder was too much to hang on to, and he lost him. Austerley sailed off and clattered hard into the zombie. The zombie fell and Austerley landed on top of him, pinning the entranced man underneath. The zombie was on his back and began to bite Austerley.

"Argh! Get the… Churchy!"

Kirkgordon dropped to a knee and fired a bolt into the leg of the zombie. But it made no difference and the affected man kept biting Austerley. Kirkgordon ran closer and hit the zombie with a hard punch that knocked its head to the floor. He went out cold.

"Shit! Is he dead?"

"How should I know?" asked Austerley. "Who cares, he was attacking me."

Sam raced up to the zombie and placed a hand on its neck. Looking at her, Kirkgordon pleaded with his eyes for a positive result.

"I can't feel anything, Kirky. I don't know."

There was a sound behind them, and Kirkgordon saw more zombies in the corridor. But he then looked back at the dead man beneath him.

"We need to go, Kirky. Now!" yelled Sam.

Instinct took over and he hauled Austerley to his feet. Seeing he could stand, he told Austerley to run and pushed Sam on her way. Then he called "Fire!" With a flaming bolt he lit up the corridor beyond the body of the zombie and caused a fire sending the other zombies scurrying.

He gave the zombies face one last lingering look and then turned. *Shit!* And he started to run.

Finding another stairwell, they went up as high as they could go finding themselves one deck from the top. Here there was the restaurant with the glass roof, tables still out but crockery and glassware was strewn everywhere. Zombies were roaming the room so Kirkgordon decided to break a glass pane at the door. This gave access to the outside of the glass, and he fired a grappling bolt up high and heard the roof shatter as the hooks pierced the glass. Making sure the rope was secure, he told Austerley to climb up, followed by Sam.

The shattering of the glass had attracted the zombies' attention, and he fired off several bolts, knocking them over, hopefully with non-fatal shots. Hearing Sam call that she was on the roof, he clambered up himself, and they traversed the glass ceiling to the other side of the vessel. Telling his party to lie low on the glass, he fired another rope down to the island below. This time he was hoping the grapple would pierce the ground before opening out, and secure tight to the ground.

After waiting for the grapple to fall, he pulled back with his arm and found a tension. But it was a hell of a drop. Breaking the glass around one of the steel framing bars of the roof, he was able to tie the rope to it, leaving slack for the movement of the vessel.

"You can't be serious?" asked Austerley. "We'll race down there at a suicidal rate."

"Look, the lagoon, Indy. You need to fall into the lagoon. Undo your belt."

Austerley did as told, and Kirkgordon bound one side with the buckle to one wrist and then looped the belt over the rope. The other wrist he wrapped tight but made sure it could come free.

"Okay, you're good."

"How am I good?" shouted Austerley.

The roof beside them shattered as gunfire began. Kirkgordon kicked Austerley on his way, and the large man screamed as he slid fast along the line to the island. Kirkgordon didn't wait to see if he was alright but instead told Sam to stand. He wrapped an arm around her, and she lifted her legs, clutching herself tight to him, burying her face in his chest, arms gripping his shoulders.

He jumped off the glass roof and fired a grappling rope over the established line to the surface. For a moment they fell freely before his arm was pulled hard and the grapple caught the line. He felt little pain in his prosthetic arm but he felt Sam dig her nails in as she felt the whip of catching the line. Glass shattered all around them but they were hurtling down, faster than he had ever gone in his life.

22

The Bridge

Havers faced the large windows of the ship's bridge, his back to the people who were holding him on the bridge. Although bound and having at least one, if not two, guns trained on him, he was calm and detached. In fact, he was in a very good place.

These few months have been so intense, so charged, searching for Farthington, he thought, *this was good, being back and doing my job. When that dragon killed Ohlos, there was no option, there had to be revenge. And I have been to the back of beyond for him, followed him through the weirdest places, only to wind up back here, in my world, looking to stop people from breaking it up again. This is my place, this is home.*

As he mulled over the recent past, Havers heard someone enter the bridge, giving an update on a search that had been initiated once he had been found.

"Did you find anything?" asked the ship's renegade Master.

"Panis is dead," said a new voice. "Found him in a box along the corridor, on the way to the bridge. He was bent double, taken out without a mess. I'd watch that one."

"Anything else?"

"Yes, a woman hiding in a ventilation recess. Ship's librarian. I called the boss about it, and she's been taken to him. Apparently he needs some sort of sacrifice for what's ahead. Seems the zombies are a bit slower than he anticipated."

The ship's new Master laughed. "Sacrifices and ancient power. Still he's paying the bills so let's keep it tight. Do another sweep in case there's any of our captive's friends still lingering."

Havers felt the emotion rising inside as he heard of Hannah's capture. *That's not good, but she's still alive. I need to regroup, as the mission remains, stop Dr Howard's plans. But I'll need to get Hannah back. Hopefully Kirkgordon will still be around and causing problems. He's sloppy and his conscience comes to the fore too often for my liking, but he seems to get the job done. And we'll need Austerley. Someone to put the cat back in the bag if it comes to it.*

Staring out of the window, he saw the water begin to move alongside the ship. It was in turmoil, beginning to turn over and over as vast quantities seemed to be displaced. The vessel rolled gently and then a large wave from the upset made the ship coup over.

The cries from the crew told him how much they had been upset by the sudden motion, but then he saw land bursting up through the ocean surface and the vessel was knocked, the ship listing badly to one side. The bridge floor went from under him, and he toppled. But he was always ready for something, and Havers managed to roll in a sort of controlled fashion.

In the confusion, he dropped a small blade from his mouth, one that lay discrete in the lining of the orifice. Twisting so that his hands now lay over the top of the blade, he picked it up, ignoring the pain that the sharp implement was causing. His ropes were cut through easily with the blade, and his hands contorted and then were free. A quick sweep to his feet cut his bonds.

Looking around, he saw the bridge in disarray as guards and crewmen struggled to regain their feet. Havers spat a few small items out of his mouth. Leaping up, he balanced precariously as the ship lurched again. One guard reacted quickly pulling his hand gun and lifting it towards Havers. A small blade cut his throat, causing a whistling sound and then gurgles in the moments after. *Good throw Arthur, still got it.*

Havers lashed out at a guard as he ran past him and made for the corridor he had come from when he entered the bridge. As he got to the door he saw a number of guards re-orientating themselves further down the passageway and decided this was too much of a hindrance. *Too easy to get caught in a narrow corridor with that number in it.*

Turning back, he struck a rising guard and grabbed the man's automatic weapon, without a break in his motion, he sprayed the front windows of the bridge with bullets, shattering them, before turning the gun onto the occupants of the bridge. He saw some fall, splattered about, some diving for cover and one flee the bridge completely. Without stopping the firing, he ran towards the bridge windows, dropping the gun just as he reached them. With a leap, he grabbed the top of the window frame and swung himself up, like a gymnast on the uneven bars. Continuing the rotation, he found his feet hitting the bridge roof and the movement finished less gracefully as he scrabbled the rest of his body onto the new level.

His hands began to scream at him, and he saw blood dripping from them where the glass had sliced into him. But there was no time to deal with that. Briefly, as he righted himself, he caught the view of an island paradise now lodged seemingly under the ship. There flashes of green and blue, vegetation and buildings. But it was all in a glance.

Turning for the opposite side of the bridge, he ran hard across one of the highest points on the vessel and looked only to the approaching edge. Beyond he saw the vast ocean, waves rippling away from the island, its emergence still causing more than a ripple. That sea would be hard to swim in, but he needed to get to the island. His next play would be there.

As the edge approached, he focused on his form and took the last step as a hop, both feet together as he left the ship. Arms flung out, he almost glided before he rotated, slowly turning until his head was approaching the sea. His arms extended, he prayed his timing was right or else his arms could break, or even his head. And then water.

It rushed past him as he entered, jarring his hands, but it was a dive he would have been proud of from any board at any pool. His speed slowing, he was able to turn and swim back to the surface. But as he broke through, he felt a surge, and he was taken back under with only half a breath as the current from the disturbance of the island dragged him down.

Do not panic. Hold your breath, releasing gradually. Havers didn't fight it, instead awaiting a moment when the current would free him. It was hard to orientate in the rush of water, but he knew that when it stopped, he'd find the pressure telling him which way to go. It was always harder to swim down. His hands began to sting and he realised the salt water was biting at the cuts they had received.

It seemed a long time, but he was finally freed from the pull of the ocean and kicked with his feet, pushing back up to the surface. On breaking through, he looked around seeing that the ship was now a reasonable distance away but still looked like a behemoth compared to the recently arrived land. Fortunately, although he had moved quite a distance, he had seemed to almost circumnavigate the land and he was less than half a mile from the shore. He saw a rocky outcrop of a beach ahead and decided to make for it.

Havers prided himself on his fitness and his wiry figure was a lot stronger than most people would have given him credit for. Without giving himself a moment to rest, he began to swim towards the shore. Who knew if anyone would follow with a rescue craft or launch from the ship? The longer he was in the water, the longer he was exposed. On the brighter side, no one would have seen his journey, what with him being swept away by the water. And now, well, he was probably out of their sight, for a short time away. He imagined confusion in the short term, and then a resumption of their key objectives. He was not one of those. He was unaware of Dr Howard before this episode. But the good doctor could rest assured, he would know the name of Havers by the end of it.

They mentioned sacrifice, he thought as he swam. *Hannah as a sacrifice. That makes sense. This kind of power to move islands usually demands a trade-off of some sort. And people always ask what is the value of a human life? Seeing what it is usually traded for, I'd say it was bloody expensive.*

23

Island Structures

Sam was gripping him as tight as he had ever been. As they descended rapidly along the makeshift death slide he had rigged up, he felt no pain from his arm at the point where the rope emerged from his limb. However, he thought his shoulder was going to pop, such was the pain. His other arm also ached from holding Sam.

The island was approaching fast, and he could see the small patch of blue he had initially seen growing fast until it was starting to fill his vision. Austerley was ahead, and he had dropped crashing into the blue causing a sensational splash. And now he applied a thought to his arm which cut the rope that held Sam and himself. Rotating as they fell, Kirkgordon's backside smacked into the water first.

He was engulfed by warm water, bubbles streaming past his face. Sam had broken the hold and drifted off from him. As he was able to fight to the surface, he quickly looked around for her but then saw a figure emerging from the lagoon they were in. *Well, that's not Austerley's arse.* Breaking his mind from what had been a sweet view, he hunted for Austerley and saw a large body floating on the other side of the small lagoon. Swimming hard over to him, he found the large man on his back, reciting something. It was in a language Kirkgordon didn't understand, but that could be anything beyond English.

"Are you okay?"

"What…, yes. But I didn't appreciate that."

"Well sorry, last time I put you on a rope slide, you where unconscious, and it was a damn sight easier. Anyway, get up and stop gibbering. We need to move and maintain our advantage."

"What advantage?" asked Austerley.

"Well, we got here first. That means you can get to the source and stop it before they can use it."

"Do you ever understand anything? Just stop it, Indy, just stop it. I don't even begin to understand it yet. I have some small pieces of information that barely gets me the history, never mind how the island works, and you just want me to stop it? If someone had actually taken the right documents from Dr Howard's office we might be ahead. But they didn't, and we're not ahead of the game. We barely know what the game is. I might as well be watching rugby for all I understand about what's happening."

"Okay," said Kirkgordon, his hands waving at Austerley to slow this tirade, "but can we get out of this damn lagoon. Speeches can wait." With that, he turned around and swam off to where Sam had exited the water.

As he clambered onto the soil at the edge of the lagoon, he noticed the strange plants, green and tall, vast shoots and purple flowers high above. The air was oppressive, a sudden change from that on the deck and there was a mist all around, seemingly from water evaporating off the surface. Ahead, Sam was in her underwear, wringing out her top and trousers.

She smiled as she saw him approach. "I thought it best to wring them out as I doubt they will dry easily in this humidity."

"Good idea," said Kirkgordon.

"I'm not sure it will work though."

"Me neither. But it's still a good idea."

She laughed and watched him stare. She was bruised here and there, some cuts across her skin, but still she had a warmness about her. She was not catwalk model, but then when did he ever want a woman like that? She looked like a real woman, with all her scratches, marks and straggly blond hair that was starting to go frizzy in the heat. Yes, a real woman. Just gorgeous.

"Hey," said Sam suddenly serious, "shouldn't we get on the move? I'd love to just sit and enjoy the view too, but those guys will probably come after us."

"You're right," conceded Kirkgordon. "But they won't come after us, they'll go to the source of whatever it is that Dr Howard wants. There were some buildings I could see briefly from the ship, so that's probably the place to begin."

A series of splashes and then the sound of someone else dripping made Kirkgordon turn to see Austerley staggering out onto the soil. He looked like a drowned rat in his now dripping Hawaiian shirt and shorts. Kirkgordon watched the large man look up, see Sam and then Kirkgordon, and then just shake his head.

Stripping now, Kirkgordon wrung his own clothes out quickly before redressing, somewhat awkwardly as items stuck to his arms and legs. When Sam grabbed his trousers to help pull them up, he jumped as her hand touched his hips from behind. When he turned around and saw her holding her jumper, asking for help putting it on, he gladly assisted. Even Austerley's tut into the air couldn't dissuade him.

The party began its next journey with Austerley agreeing that the buildings were the best course of action. The vegetation around them was dense and also a strange combination of what normally passed for land and sea plants. There were incredibly large patches of a brown seaweed type plant that went "pop" whenever you stood on one of its yellow pods. Kirkgordon was reminded of "bladder wrack" but this was a lot noisier and hence he asked everyone to refrain from stepping on it.

There were large, cucumber-shaped plants, purple in colour and with tiny hairs on their skin. Another plant had orange fruit seemingly hanging from it. And there were also large rushes that packed tight together, making the group's path more often than not obscured. After securing an initial line of sight to the buildings, Kirkgordon used the sun and the massive cruise liner behind them to keep on track.

Although first onto the island, it was doubtful they would have much of a time advantage over Dr Howard's party when they came. Kirkgordon also wondered what size of party he would bring. Would he need an army of sorts with him or would it just be the closest advisors?

The exertions of the previous night were also taking their toll, and he found the going difficult despite the fact that every time he looked at Sam she flashed that wonderful smile of hers. Although enjoying her being with him, he was worried for her safety. *I have some sort of ability to look after myself, Austerley is capable of bringing down the world, but Sam, what does she have to protect her? This isn't a world for her.*

Kirkgordon had insisted on Austerley bringing up the rear to keep Sam safe in the middle of the group, but he was dropping back all too often. Standing time and again waiting for the staggering man, he saw him suffer in the moist air, the damned heat making it seem like cold had never been part of life's rich tapestry. Was the foot also acting up? Austerley was hobbling to a degree.

But he seemed determined nonetheless, probably due to the new weirdness that confronted them. There was a part of Austerley that was like a child with a new toy, and during brief moments when Kirkgordon saw him catch his breath, the child emerged, muttering about what they might find. Not that much of it made sense to Kirkgordon.

At last they broke through the vegetation to arrive beside a building that seemed built of a clay-type material, although Kirkgordon doubted this to be so, as underwater travel surely required something more robust. There was a door, or rather a doorway, just an opening in the side of the building. The building itself was only the size of a garden shed, and Kirkgordon approached it with caution, moving in from the blindside of the door.

There was no sound from the interior, and the island itself had a lack of birdsong or other background animal noises, making the place seem eerie, like a bizarre ghost town. Juking his head briefly inside, Kirkgordon found an empty space with a green lichen on the walls that glowed, lighting up the space to a partial extent. There were dark corners, but the main dimensions could be seen.

Sam broke off from behind, amazed at the light and went to wander into the building, but Kirkgordon pulled her back.

"We don't know what's in there, Sam. Let Austerley look first. He also has an antenna for these things."

"Where does he keep it?" Sam asked.

"No. A sense of them, an antenna sense."

Sam smiled, and he realised she was winding him up. Kirkgordon smiled back, but he knew what statements like that meant in these kind of situations. She was at best nervous, more likely scared heading towards terrified.

Looking inside, Austerley seemed pleased. He stood drinking in all he could see before turning to Kirkgordon and giving that "superior knowledge" face Kirkgordon had seen many times.

"Well, I doubt you would have gotten very far as that language on the floor is not from earth. This is an entrance to the main structure."

"How is it an entrance?" asked Sam, "It's just a room."

"Until you press the switch. The language on the floor is a common tongue, which has been seen in many strange places around the world. It is detailing the route to the main buildings which are over there." Austerley pointed off in the general direction they had been travelling.

"A secret entrance on so small an island?" queried Kirkgordon. "That makes me think the main entrance is a trap. We need to be careful, this could be booby trapped. So how do we access the way in?"

"Like this," said Austerley and stepped inside, took two steps to the left and smacked his foot on the ground. The floor descended beside him, a circular piece that fanned out as it descended, creating a staircase into the ground beneath.

"Wow," said Sam," this is crazy."

Just you wait, thought Kirkgordon, *we ain't got to crazy quite yet.*

Stepping forward, Kirkgordon took the lead as he tiptoed

down the stairs that proceeded in their downward spiral for what he thought to be about twenty to twenty-five metres. The green lichen now became a better light as what daylight had penetrated the building on the surface was gone and the plant on the wall seemed to glow all the more because of it. As he reached the foot of the stairwell, he saw a long corridor in front of them with markings on the floor.

"Austerley, you're up. What do they say?"

There was a tight squeezing past as Austerley approached from the rear and then dropped to his knees looking at the markings on the floor.

"Well, it's not one of my fifty languages that I am proficient in."

"Fifty!" said Sam. Kirkgordon held his finger to his mouth, indicating she should be quiet.

"…but there are some similar elements to others I have seen. I'm not certain, but there's a general implication of death in this writing."

"Death? That's it? Indy, everywhere we go there's a general implication of death. Do you mean death here, in the corridor, or death in a more widespread sense?"

"Well," mused Austerley, "it could be both. But I think this corridor may be booby-trapped. Although…" He stepped forward and slammed his foot on a piece of ground with marks on it. The walls began to move at the sides and Sam clung tight to Kirkgordon. "It's okay," said Austerley, "I'm just making it wider."

The corridor did widen to about twenty feet across before stopping. It seemed endless looking down it and there were now darker patches as the green lichen plant had more space to illuminate. Kirkgordon peered down the sides and saw that it wasn't a solid wall down the corridor but rather there were gaps in the sides. Sometimes there were holes, sometimes whole sections of a few feet missing.

"Are we okay to go on?" asked Kirkgordon.

"Should be, just stay alert."

Taking Sam by the hand, Kirkgordon began to walk forward, gingerly at first before becoming more assured. He glanced this way and that, scanning for anything untoward. Sam was tight on his heels, and he could hear Austerley hobbling on the stone floor behind him. *Good, this seems alright, just a simple corridor to walk down. Maybe the death's further ahead.*

He saw it move in the corner of his vision. One of the larger gaps in the side wall had something emerging from it, coming straight at his side. Kirkgordon reared back as two spears drove out from the wall side and passed right in front of him. There was also a blur of white and he was caught on the side by something blunt.

He fell, spinning backwards away from the danger. Sam screamed and Kirkgordon quickly got to his feet, desperate to see his opponent. Before him, jutting out from the gap in the wall were two spears, one head high and the other about knee height. They were sharp but rusty. And on them was a skeleton.

He took Sam in his arms, turning her face from the sight but something intrigued him. He could see Austerley peering, almost in delight. The skeleton was clean and white, almost looking perfect like a laboratory specimen. But this skeleton was different. This skeleton was not human.

24

Multiple Targets

The rocky outcrop turned out to be quite sharp, and Havers had to pick a route through the craggy edge that was being lapped by the sea. It seemed to be a black rock, made from what he didn't know, but it was able to cut easily. Once ashore, he discovered a crumbly soil and dense vegetation beyond, with an array of plants and shoots that had some of the strangest colours, like beetroot was the rule when it came to vegetable colouring and not the exception.

With the current having taken him far off track, Havers wondered about his next move and so climbed a purple tree to consider his options. Did he make his way to the buildings he had seen farther inland, or did he circle the shore to reach the ship and hopefully intercept Dr Howard's party as they came ashore? He couldn't see anyone from the vessel and concluded they hadn't made their way ashore yet. Maybe they were sweeping the boat to find anyone else.

The ship loomed at the side of the island which Havers reckoned measured less than a mile across in nearly every direction. Striking out through the intense vegetation, he believed he would be shielded from general view, especially as his natural habit, instilled by years of practice, was to pick a path that obscured his presence by staying close to larger objects. The island made this easy.

Whilst the vegetation may have been to his liking, Havers disliked the extreme humidity he was experiencing. Steam was rising off the island and making his journey uncomfortable. *There must be an inner core of heat, or maybe the island has risen from close into the earth's surface, but then there would be no vegetation.* The puzzle was confusing until Havers thought about the power source, whatever it was, that Dr Howard was seeking. *That power may be causing the heat, and the island has been drenched. We are just at the top of the kettle.*

As he neared the ship, he saw a gangplank being manoeuvred, making a pathway from a door in the vessel to the ground below. Settling down amidst a shrub of dark blue, he watched proceedings as a string of people emerged from the boat. First came a number of bodyguards, all carrying automatic weapons, and who took up flanking positions around the gangway. Next came a large number of zombies followed by a dark skinned woman in a dress that surely had been damaged in some way, given its poor attempt to cover her up.

Although stumbling and looking ravenous for action, the zombies seemed to be held in a mental check, possibly coming from the woman. On reaching the bottom of the gangway, the zombies raced into the undergrowth about two hundred metres from the plank's end and began to tear through every shrub and plant. Havers was further back, but he made plans on where to move to if the time came. However, the zombies quickly returned back to the dark-skinned woman.

A middle aged man then appeared with a beard and Panama

hat, dressed in a white suit. He took a look at the preparations made around him, giving a nod before four large men, each well over six-foot-tall, flanked him, and the small group made their way onto the island. And then he saw another group come out, a group of women who clearly weren't zombies but who were tied together by a single rope and escorted by a number of guards.

Priorities, Arthur, priorities. One, stop Dr Howard from accessing this power whatever it is. That overrides everything. Second, free those hostages on the rope. Three, turn everyone back to human from being a zombie. Four, get the ship away from here and to general help. Three and four may be interchangeable and four may already be on the way. How many hostages? Two, four, six, eight...,

Hannah was there. Right at the rear of the party, but Havers found himself having to remind himself to stay hidden and stay calm. Even from this distance, it was clear they had tortured her in some regard. Her face was heavily bruised and her clothing was torn. *They will pay for that. And if they have interfered with her...I will castrate the bastards.*

Recognising the anger building up within him, Havers started to breathe easily and deeply, seeking a calmer state. Years of working this job had taught him that extreme emotion didn't get the results that were needed. Only cool and calm heads ever sorted anything. But this was Hannah. She was blood. Family was family. Hers had been his after his parents had passed on. Although, they were always family anyway, his father having instilled the importance of the unit in society, the backbone of being British. Family stuck together, family looked out for each other.

But the party from the boat was on the move, and Havers began to track from a distance, his eyes rarely leaving Hannah.

162

That was until he caught a flash of something beyond the party. It was brief but it was careless. It was like the glimmer from a blade in strong sunlight. Whether this was accurate he didn't know, but it was from something man made, certainly not of the island.

His interest sufficiently peaked, he routed around the rear of the ship's party and sought out whatever had made the flash. But he was cautious. Who was to say there was only one person? There may be a number of interlopers.

It almost caught him unaware. Right across his path strode an Asian man, only around five and a half feet tall with a balding head and a bare torso. He carried a gun in one hand and a knife in the other. Havers halted on the spot and remained motionless hoping the man didn't turn his way. And then beyond the man, someone else flanking the ship's party. She was taller, elegant like Hannah but with ebony skin and eyes that clashed through the night-like skin, reminding him of an owl as the bird opened its eyes to see. She wore only a crop top which Havers was beginning to see as a sensible option in this humid cauldron.

But what struck him about the two people, different as they were, was that on their right arms, both had a tattoo. His was etched in black and hers in white but they were the same. A trident being held aloft with seaweed around it. *Curious, another party enters the fray.* And then they were off, soundlessly moving through the undergrowth.

Havers remained still, wary of others. And his patience was rewarded as he caught glimpses of what appeared to be an Eastern European giant, well over six foot, and another woman, with a complexion that spoke of the South Seas. *This show gets more interesting by the minute.* He couldn't see if they

163

had tattoos as they both had long sleeves on, but he was sure they were from the same group.

Dr Howard's group maintained a rigid pace and path towards the settlements at the rear of the island. As they approached, Havers saw ornate figures adorning what looked like clay walls. There was a Poseidon-like figure complete with trident. Several fish were caught in relief on the walls and he saw mermaids, bare and alluring. Most figures had some sort of crown or a ring of seaweed on them, indicating some degree of standing as far as Havers could guess.

The vegetation broke as the main party reached the building and Havers from his remote location could see stone steps leading into an entrance hall of some sort. There was general milling about as Hannah and her group were being brought to the front of the party. Dr Howard seemed to be talking to one of his guards, indicating that the party needed to enter the building via the steps, but that the hostages were to go first.

Havers had kept a close eye on the strange people who had been tracking the party, and he saw that the Asian man was readying himself, bringing his hand gun to the level primed to shoot. Hannah would be caught up in this. Hannah would be in the crossfire.

With a blinding pace, Havers raced through the plant life and struck the man on the neck before he could do anything. He toppled to the ground. Havers, however, wasn't making sure of any of this, instead trusting his skills as he continued to the man's colleague, the larger man. Hearing his colleague fall, the European man had turned and looked straight into Havers' eyes as he was taken to the ground where Havers hit him with a brutal punch to the temple. The man was out cold.

Again Havers rounded and caught the woman with the

ebony skin off guard as she had started to route towards her colleagues. Her legs were swept from under her and as she hit the ground, a nerve was struck in her neck rendering her unconscious. Havers then went to move to the last of the people he had seen but the girl with the South Seas' appearance was not there. Then he heard the click of a weapon right behind his head.

Spinning away he desperately sought the weapon. His eyes caught its image as it was being traced to his movement, only a foot away. His hand shot out at the woman's wrist, knocking the gun clear as it fired into the ground. There was no retort and Havers saw a silencer on the weapon. With a hand stretched out to prevent the weapon returning to him, he ducked behind his assailant and kicked her hard behind the knee, forcing her to drop down. He then swung an arm around her neck and began to choke her.

The woman tried to swing the gun around but Havers had a hand on her wrist and locked it out tight so the weapon remained clear of him at all times. As she began to suffer from the choke hold, she dropped the gun and grabbed at his arm. But he held tight, and the woman soon succumbed so he let her slip to the ground.

Maybe he should have dispatched them, but he was not sure that they were the enemy amidst this confusion. Indeed, they may be useful later. He turned his attention back to Dr Howard's party and to Hannah. But all he saw was her back disappearing with the other hostages as they entered the building alone.

25

The Passage

"That's not a human skeleton," said Kirkgordon.

"Obviously," responded Austerley, stepping in closer to the remains hung on the spear combination that had emerged from the wall. "There's fins on it, and the sleekness of the design. The head has a point to it, like a fish, and the feet are frankly fascinating. There's a foot within a foot. Actually a foot within a flipper probably. Look at how the bones splay out above a reasonably human foot. It's not completely the same but I think these beings could walk as well as swim."

"You mean like us?" queried Sam.

"No. Not like us at all. We don't swim, we just splash about. This creature could probably swim at least four to five times faster than us and maybe more depending on the flesh over the bone. Amazing."

Austerley went to move to the far side of the creature but Kirkgordon reached out and grabbed him. "Wait. How do you know you won't trigger any more traps?"

Looking back at him with disgust, Austerley continued

forward and knelt at the far side of the creature. He reached with his hand and traced the curves of the bones, lost in a sense of wonder. Kirkgordon placed Sam behind him and studied the floor. The light was poor, but he could see faint markings. There was a curly swirl, a triangular feature, a wave-like image, a forest and many more. He felt Sam leaning over him, and she gasped as she saw the vague images on the floor.

"Austerley, what do you make of the patterns on the floor?" asked Kirkgordon.

"Where?"

Kirkgordon pointed down and watched the large man bend close to the floor before moving away again. "Hard to read in this light."

"What did we stand on to activate the spears?" Kirkgordon looked at his own feet. *There's a swirl and a forest in his area. Could it be that simple?*

"I think you stood on the tree like shape," said Sam. "We should avoid the tree shape." She was gripping tight to Kirkgordon, her body trembling. *It was probably a little excitement mixed in with fear*, thought Kirkgordon as he knew the feeling well. *There's always a rush that accompanies the horror.*

"I really should collect this specimen."

"What?" Kirkgordon was shocked. "Indy, we're in the middle of death trap dungeon and in a race to stop a man from who knows what sort of power, and you want to start building up the laboratory? Get your eyes off the skeleton and onto the floor. Is Sam right saying we avoid the trees?"

"I don't know. Her hypothesis is sound except why not avoid the curly signs too? Who knows what the words mean? I don't...yet."

167

Kirkgordon turned to Sam. "Stay a few feet behind me. I'll step it out, and Austerley and you will just have to walk in my footsteps." Sam nodded but was reluctant to let go. But she gave a look of resignation and dropped back. "Indy, heads up, we're moving on."

Kirkgordon peered at the floor, carefully stepping onto a triangular shape before moving to a wave shape next. He then found a shape with criss-crossing lines before hoping back to a wave. Moving out to the right hand side of the corridor, he managed to keep clear of the swirls and the forests.

"Churchy, did you look up at all? Where you were standing, did you look up?"

"Busy here, Indy."

"Yes, but did you look up?" Austerley's voice was wavering. "I think you should have looked up."

Turning around, Kirkgordon looked back and above where Austerley was standing. There was a faint light emanating, almost imperceptible, right above where he had stood originally. He watched in horror as Sam, spotting the light above the original spot, moved away, backed towards the other wall and walked right under another faint light source.

"Sam, stop," shouted Kirkgordon. "Don't move."

"Too late," said Austerley, "she's under it."

There was a sound of rushing water and walls began to move in from behind Austerley.

"Sam, here," said Kirkgordon, reaching for her hand as she sprang towards him. Austerley also stood and began backing to Kirkgordon.

"Sounds like water, Churchy. Lots of water." A hole opened above them in the ceiling.

"Run! Just run!" yelled Kirkgordon taking Sam by the

hand and tearing off down the corridor. He didn't wait for Austerley as he heard water hitting the floor behind him. Sam was pulling his arm back, being considerably slower, and Kirkgordon could only see more corridor ahead. And then the water was passing by his feet, the sound of an ocean roaring behind him, spurring him on. He heard Austerley cry out, and he was hit by a wall of water lifting him off his feet.

His hand gripped Sam's as tightly as he could, and he fought to find the rest of her as he was driven along the corridor. He felt her body beside his leg and reached out to wrap his legs around her. A hand grabbed his inner thigh, and he felt nails scrabbling at his flesh. The water was beginning to have a more concerted flow and was throwing them about less, but the general force was pushing them onward. His head broke from the mass of water to be only two feet from the ceiling and he gasped at the air.

Glancing down the corridor, he saw the water seemingly disappearing into the floor, the corridor continuing beyond. He had no time to think but instead thought a hook bolt onto his crossbow arm and took a quick shot at the ceiling beyond where the water was disappearing. He saw the hook explode into rock, prayed it had bitten and thought the rope to wind in on his arm. He went over the waterfall and felt the tension on the rope suddenly go tight.

With one hand on Sam and his legs wrapped around her body, he felt the strain in the shoulder of his crossbow arm. Just as he felt it might separate, he realised they were moving up. Hope grew in him, and he wondered how far they might have to go. And then his face felt a foot kick it, and the rope suddenly became even heavier.

A raw pain gripped his shoulder and the mechanism pulling

them up could be heard straining through the noise of the water. But they were moving up, and he realised there was Austerley, bent around the rope above him, the water pushing the Professor against the rope. Kirkgordon then felt himself start to rub against a wall and realised they were reaching the top of the waterfall. Hopefully the stupid arse above him was conscious and could pull himself up.

It seemed an age before his head broke out of water again but as it did the rope above felt lighter, the pain in his shoulder eased, and he felt his arm start to turn onto a surface. His back ached as he rolled over the lip of the dry side of the drop of the waterfall but he kept his legs tight around Sam. She was moving and only when he had been dragged well clear of the drop did he instruct his arm to cut the rope.

Collapsing onto his back, he heard Sam cough and splutter, and then her hands moved up from his thigh, across his chest and found his cheeks. She planted a deep and enthusiastic kiss on him. And then another one. And another.

"A little help here," said a voice behind him, "or are you just going to chew the face off each other?"

Sam sat up, and Kirkgordon opened his eyes to see her on top of him pushing back her hair. She was breathless, soaked through, and he reckoned at this exact moment in time, possibly one of the best sights a man could ever see.

"Don't listen to him, Sam," said Kirkgordon, reaching up and pulling her down again to resume their interaction. They broke off a few more excited kisses and she lay on top of him, both exhausted but sharing a moment.

It was Austerley who stood up first, and Kirkgordon could hear him wandering off beyond where they were lying.

"Indy, wait up." The water had seemingly subsided, a blast

that had swept them along and had intended to flush them out. But they were still in one piece. His shoulder was sore, even when he had reached up for Sam, it had hurt. She rolled off him, and he turned his head to watch her lying on her back. Her womanly curves rose and fell as she breathed, and he found himself not wishing to go anywhere. And yet he barely even knew her.

Hearing Austerley continue to move off, Kirkgordon stood up and let his good arm linger for Sam to pull herself up. She kissed him again when they were standing, before taking a good look at his face.

"I thought we were dead."

"Shush, you can't think. It just gets in the way at times like this. You have to believe and just keep going. We are a long way from safe."

Sam nodded and took his hand. He had no idea if they really meant anything to each other or if this was just the drama of the moment. Or was he just lonely after his other relationships were broken? But he didn't care. She was here, he was here. So for now, they were together.

Austerley was a little way ahead and suddenly seemed to become agitated as he dripped along the floor. Without warning, Austerley disappeared to the left.

"Indy, wait up," shouted Kirkgordon, running forward with Sam holding his hand.

"This is amazing, just fascinating. I have never seen such a sight." Austerley was ecstatic and Kirkgordon wondered what he had seen.

Rounding the corner into a small room, Kirkgordon saw Austerley amongst a pile of bones that were knee deep in the corner.

"What the hell's the excitement?" asked Kirkgordon as Sam hid her head in his chest at the sight.

"There's at least two dozen different sets of bones here. From many different places, dimensions, worlds, call them what you will. And most are intact. It's amazing."

"Hang on. You say there's a load of bones of things from other worlds, all in this small room. Why? Why are they here? This room? Unless…"

Kirkgordon heard the gap at the door close as a wall filled the opening, turning the room dark.

26

Trials

Hannah was shaking as she climbed the clay steps at the entrance to the building. Across from her, she saw the sharp teeth on the face of a fish creature with a giant tail, held in relief on the wall. The snarl showing was almost jumping out at her from the wall as she walked forward with the other twenty or so women from the ship.

The air was humid, so much so she had opened her company shirt and tied it by rolling the end on either side and tying it in the middle. The sleeves were also rolled up, but still the air was oppressive, and she was sweating intensely. Her black librarian trousers had the dark soil of the island around the edges and she had long since discarded her high heels, walking in her bare feet, often immersed in the warm soil.

Arthur was also missing. Since he had asked her to remain in the large vent fixture, she hadn't seen him and it was playing on her mind. After he had disappeared on mission, in that far off world, the family and her had fought with the realisation he was not coming home, that efficient, determined Arthur was no longer saving the world. It hadn't seemed a reality.

And now, just as she was embracing the joy of his survival, he was gone again. There had been gunfire. She knew no more.

After she had been found by one of the guards, she had been manhandled and thrown into a room with other women who had not turned into the zombie state. They had been subjected to a group of guards who tortured them with the idea of not just physical harm, but who had also talked about which one of the women they would be entertaining that night, and not in the take-out-to-dinner fashion.

When the dark-skinned woman had walked in and obviously commanded the guards to get the women on the move, it had been a relief, until Hannah had seen the wildness in her eyes. Although not having been a field agent for long, she could see the influence of something else, something manic in the mind, a woman tapped into a region normal people did not entertain.

The steps were steep and the other women with her were huddled as the guards shouted at them to move up and into the building. One woman fell and was shouted at by a guard who then walked towards her, automatic weapon pointed. Another woman grabbed her as she sobbed and hauled the woman back into the group.

Inside the building, Hannah's eyes struggled to adjust to a dark hallway. There were statues flanking the entrance but she struggled to see what they were. Before her on the floor was an imprint in the ground, depicting strange creatures in the throes of death, horrible in their variety. There were markings as well, presumably a language judging by the repetitiveness of certain characters, maybe detailing what to do. But it was as lost on Hannah as it was on the other women despite her linguistic skills. Maybe Austerley would be able to understand it.

One woman walked a little ahead of the group. Red haired and in her later years, she was still dressed in a fashionable evening gown, although her hair and make-up were now a mess, having suffered from a crying face and the extreme humidity. Bare footed, she hitched her dress up past her knees as she turned this way and that, almost stumbling along, like a child in a hall of mirrors. And then the floor gave way.

In an instant she was gone. Her screams reverberated around the hallway, causing panic amongst the women, some of whom turned and fled from the building. Hannah stopped in her tracks as her eyes became adjusted to the light and scanned the floor where the woman had fallen. There was a hole just big enough for a person but the surrounding floor looked strong. And on the floor were markings, different patterns and pictures.

From behind came the screams of women who had exited and who were now being forcibly returned to the hallway. A guard was grunting and pointing a gun at a woman's head.

"You!" he shouted at a young female crew member, "you walk along, get to the other side or I will blow her brains out." As if to reinforce the idea, he hit the woman's head with the end of his gun and then looked at the girl.

The girl screamed as her mind calculated the horror before her. When she saw the guard hit the woman's head again, she turned and ran down the hallway. Just beyond where the red headed woman had fallen through the floor, another piece gave way, and she hurtled out of sight.

Hannah could feel the panic building but she was also trying to breathe methodically and calm her mind, not an easy task as the women around her shrieked and wailed. *Think Hannah, think girl. What would Arthur do? How do you save these women who are tumbling to their doom?* As another woman was pushed forward, Hannah tried to ignore her and study the floor ahead.

There must be a way across because otherwise, why bother? There has to be a simple route, something that meant those in the know could come and go, or at least gain access. But what? Another cry from a falling woman threatened to break her concentration but she persisted. *The patterns around the holes must be good. Underneath there would be some sort of stanchion and they would have marked the top, thereby making a path. But what symbols?*

The guard suddenly grabbed Hannah, his face thrust into hers as he seemed to smell her. She felt violated as he looked her up and down, almost licking his lips.

"Shame to waste you in a drop out here. You'd be better in my cabin tonight." He grabbed her hair pulling her close and sniffed her neck before forcibly kissing her. "No, not you yet."

He broke off and forced another woman to start a walk along the dangerous hallway. The frightened blonde haired woman closed her eyes as she walked, quivering and sobbing before her release from the terror as she fell, exposing another part of the hallway.

"I want her to do it!" The voice was strong, commanding and new in the hallway. It was followed by a parting of guards and captive women, breaking to allow the dark skinned woman who had come into their room earlier, to break through. Wearing what could only be described as bare essentials, Hannah saw the same wild look in her eye from before but now there was genuine excitement.

"You have been watching and you have been calm. Even when that brute took hold of you, there was an inner resolve. Not a snivelling excuse for a woman like these others. No, I

176

think you may have it, the strength of the female species, the mother to be one day. A woman who can do what it takes, whatever it takes to stay alive, to keep her brood alive. A woman who could kill if necessary. A woman like myself."

I am nothing like you, thought Hannah.

"Oh but you are, child, more than you think."

How did she hear me?

"Surprised that I read you? Ha! You'll grow into this strength you see before you, be my protégé, and maybe be even more." The woman touched Hannah's cheek, delicately, almost affectionately, but again Hannah felt like she was being looked at, desired. "What is your name child?"

"Hannah." Without looking at her, Hannah stared impassively like a soldier giving their rank.

"From the Hebrew, is it not? Favour, grace. Well, you have found my favour, child. Do you know my name?" Hannah shook her head. "My name is Nepthys, Mictecacihuatl, Tia, Camazotz, Maman Brigitte, or you can just take your pick. I am the Goddess of Death and I have chosen you. Walk now my child, walk to your doom. Or maybe you walk to my arms, to languish on my bed with me. But walk!"

Hannah felt spooked. The woman had eyes that penetrated, that somehow made you stare back at her even though you were horrified by what she was saying. But nonetheless, she felt compelled to go, to walk. And it wasn't any gun making her do it.

Think Hannah, think! Look at the symbols, look at the ground, read the symbols.

Before Hannah was the large hallway, and she saw the holes where the other women had fallen. But they were a distance off and she had trouble peering at the designs beside them.

177

There's a water shape, flowing water shape. A tree like shape. The houses, the houses look safe.

Nervously she slowly placed a foot on the water symbol. Her heart stopped as she transferred her weight. But the ground held. She looked around. The house symbol, just over from her. Again she reached out with a foot delicately. The same tense feeling, the thumping of her heart in her ears and then relief.

"Good, my child," laughed the woman who called herself a goddess, "good, you are not without intelligence. It would take a wise woman to love me."

Ignore what she's saying and focus, focus! There's another house... and step... good. And now a tree, go for that tree. Easy, does it easy...that's not the same symbol!

Hannah's foot crashed through the floor and she instinctively threw herself back to the ground she had come from. Her desperate clawing was misguided, and she hit her forearms onto the ground and began to fall backwards, away from the edge. But her hand caught a chunk of ground jutting out where the surface had broken. With one hand she hung precariously. Beneath her she could hear ground crashing into water. And there came a snarl, and she felt eyes watching her from below.

Don't look down, don't. Second hand onto the hold. Get your hand up, girl. She felt herself swinging and decided to go with her motion knowing she wouldn't be able to hold it and would soon fall off. But the motion enabled her to swing her free arm up and her hand desperately grasped the jutting piece of floor.

She was praising herself for losing that extra weight last year, and with her arms feeling like the muscles would soon break through, she hauled herself back up, her bare stomach scraping on the floor edge, causing a slight bleed. Standing up, she took a breath, tried to refocus.

"Good, you have spirit, you have hunger. But where next, child? Choose carefully. Make sure of your footing."

Hannah looked around her desperately, searching for the shapes she knew were safe. Some distance away she saw the water shape. It was within reach, but it would be a jump. No gentle setting down of a foot, it would be all or nothing. She looked around her for other symbols but there were none she knew to be safe. From below the floor she heard the snarl again, and she took a moment to stare down.

Something moved, something was down there, somewhere in the dark and it did not sound friendly. Standing upright again, she drew in her breath. *Okay Hannah, this is it. Keep cool, keep calm. Focus on the landing, focus on the landing. And swing, swing and then jump. One...two...three!*

Hannah jumped.

27

The Creature in the Dark

"Sam, stay close whatever you do, stay close."

Kirkgordon felt her hand in his and pulled her close. The room was dark and what luminescence was given off by the strange lichen seemed extremely faded now. Disorientation was an issue, and Kirkgordon rooted his feet, recalling the geography of the room in his head. The door was behind him and the bones before him. *Move away from the bones.*

"Indy, step towards my voice, slowly and carefully. Away from the bones."

"But I've got one in my hand…"

"Indy, back!"

Kirkgordon moved backwards towards the door of the room and felt his shoulders touch the wall. Sam was holding him tight, but he had lost sight of Austerley, finding the light barely enough to see a hand in front of his own face. Then he heard it.

There was a hiss from the far corner. In the dark, something slithered, and the sound dredged up all thoughts of malignancy and horror. What was it?

"Something's out there. Across from us," said Sam moving even closer to Kirkgordon. Austerley's feet made a sloppy noise in the quiet as he presumably made his way back towards Kirkgordon. And then his back was inches from Kirkgordon, and he placed a finger on Austerley's back, causing him to jump.

"It's me," he whispered, "just move to my side."

Kirkgordon heard the hiss again and thought whatever it was had gone to his left. He knelt and placed his crossbow arm to the fore. His eyes peered into the utter darkness and he suddenly drew in the saltwater smell of the room. But he didn't smell the creature.

"Indy, any ideas what it is?" he said in a sullen voice.

"No, nothing definite. I don't even know what it could look like."

Kirkgordon felt Sam kneel down against him. Her hand was on his shoulder, and its trembling was transferring to him. And then something slid past his feet. Another hiss.

"God, that's close," whispered Sam.

"Argggh!" screamed Austerley.

Kirkgordon felt him slide away and dove a hand down clutching his shirt collar.

"My leg! It's got my leg."

"Argh!" screamed Sam. There was a thud in the dark and Sam groaned. Kirkgordon dropped Austerley's collar and scrabbled in the direction of Sam's scream. He tumbled over something on the floor, something that was moist as his trouser legs caught it. Sam began to yell.

"Argh, it's around my waist. Kirky, I can't breathe, it's got my stomach. It's crushing me."

181

With searching hands, Kirkgordon found Sam and the wet, thick skin that was encircling her. He pulled at it but found no purchase. Bolt. He fired at close range and felt it whistle past him. *Maybe it came back off the skin.* He fired again and this time heard Austerley cry out.

"Argh, that's my bloody leg."

"Flame," cried Kirkgordon. As the dark fled from his lighted arm, he saw a head race at him, fangs protruding from a dripping mouth. Kirkgordon flung himself aside. As he rose, the head came again, and he thought of a new plan. Made in an instant, his instinct to trust himself kicked in and he drove his arm into the mouth coming towards him. He fired a flaming bolt and then another as the mouth closed down on his arm.

The creature seemed to wail and Kirkgordon was picked up as the head shook. He was bounced here and there before the mouth opened, throwing him into a wall. But there was a fire in the room now and the smell of cooking meat, though the air was a toxic taint of gone off meat. As he lay crumpled upside down against the wall, Kirkgordon could see Sam fighting her way clear of the creature and beating it with her fists.

The head of the creature rocked a few more times and then fell limp on the ground. Kirkgordon rolled back off the wall collapsing on the ground of the small room. He felt Sam's arms on him and tried to sit up. She kissed him.

"This is becoming a habit," he said when she broke off.

"It's the only bit of this I'm enjoying."

"If the dream couple are okay, can someone see to the brains in the room," moaned Austerley.

Kirkgordon nodded at Sam, and she went over to Austerley. "His leg's collapsed in somewhat. Is this one false? It's been pretty mangled."

"Everyone wants Indy's foot," laughed Kirkgordon. He knew it wasn't really funny, but he was desperate not to think about what happened. Austerley grimaced at him and started to try to get to his feet with Sam's help. Kirkgordon saw Sam's wince as she helped him.

"Are you okay?" asked Kirkgordon.

"I've just had my leg eaten by a reptile from the deep. So no, I'm not great."

"I meant Sam, you arse. Sam, are you okay?"

Sam shook her head and clutched her stomach. Kirkgordon got up and walked over to her. In the dying firelight, he had her lie down and slowly moved her top up, revealing her stomach. With a gentle hand, he tenderly examined the skin on her stomach before moving to her sides. Watching Sam wince, he continued moving to her ribs.

"How far are you going," Sam said with a forced laugh. "Not sure this is the time and place."

"Oh, I don't know. But I need Austerley to have a go. His hands can tell more."

Austerley looked quizzical. Kirkgordon indicated that Austerley should feel Sam's stomach and he repelled.

"Indy, see if you can find anything wrong in there."

"I'm not a medical doctor. I am good but not a qualified doctor."

"I don't want your medical expertise, I want you to have a look at Sam's ribs. There's a colour there I don't think is normal. I want to know what it is."

"Oh, okay." Austerley got down on his knees, and Sam started when he touched her skin.

"Damn, those hands are freezing. Warm them up or I'll pass out from the cold."

But Austerley's face was showing a concern, and it didn't react to the humour. Carefully he drew his hands to and fro across Sam, and where Kirkgordon had been delicate and not strayed too high, Austerley had no shame in checking in and around Sam's bra.

"There's definitely something there and it's spreading," said Austerley.

"But I don't feel anything," queried Sam.

"I believe you," replied Austerley, "but there is something moving, across the flesh, something from this place. I wonder if that creature was enchanted."

"Will it kill me, this stuff that's spreading?"

Austerley shrugged his shoulders. "I don't know. The creature was alive, so that's a good thing. But it's also the only evidence I have, there's a lot I don't know about here, and I don't know how, or if it will, manifest further. I'm in the dark. But it's there; Churchy could feel it; I could sense and feel it. Maybe you can too?"

"But you can stand and walk, so we need to keep moving," Kirkgordon said, offering a hand to Sam. "Our first thought has to be, how to get out of here?"

"There's no sign that the creature only lived in here, reckon it must have been sent in when people entered. It obviously feasted and that would mean it would need more food than what's here. At least that's my hypothesis."

"Agreed, Indy. Sam, start feeling the walls with Indy and see if you can find something loose or at least, broken or something. A breath of wind, something that indicates anything beyond."

The party of three began to feel their way around the small room, painstakingly going over every piece of stone in the near

184

wall and then doing the same with the other walls. Having searched and found nothing Kirkgordon ordered them to search again. Halfway through this search, Sam spoke up.

"Above us. I think it's above us. I have an urge to go up. Around about this corner. I want to go up Kirky, I want to go up."

"Okay," answered Kirkgordon, "climb on my back." He bent down, and Sam placed her legs either side of his neck. Taking her thighs in his hands, he lifted her up to the ceiling, stopping in a slight crouch lest he bounce her head off the stones above.

Sam felt the stones above her. "Yes, there's a draught right here, very faint but definitely here. And I also want to go up here. And…where's my arm gone?"

Sam's arm had disappeared into the wall. Quickly she pulled it back out before pausing for a moment. Then she stuck her head through the wall. "There's a platform up here," she said, "and the sound of water. I want to swim. Kirky, I want to swim."

Sam was becoming excited, and Kirkgordon stood up fully. Soon, he felt her move a foot onto his shoulder and climb up off him. Austerley was looking cautiously at him, but Kirkgordon knelt down and told him to climb onto his shoulders. *Man, he's heavy. Too many times I've had to carry this guy.*

Once Austerley had climbed up off him, Kirkgordon waited to see if anyone would send back a hand. He could send a rope bolt up but his arm was feeling somewhat damaged and he'd rather find another way. Also the stones had deflected the standard bolts, so it would be a risk, especially as he couldn't see the others. Austerley's hand emerged through the ceiling.

As he was pulled up and broke the plane of the ceiling, Kirkgordon could hear water too. Rising into another dimly lit area, with the same luminous lichen he had seen before, he realised he was about to get onto a small platform. Sam was facing away from him as he climbed up, looking at a fast moving river of water that disappeared off to the right.

"Down there?" said Sam, pointing off along the river. "We go down there?" Kirkgordon looked quizzically at Austerley who just shrugged and then nodded.

"Okay," said Kirkgordon, "we go down there. Is there a raft or anything about?"

"We swim, Kirky." Sam was facing the water, and she dropped her trousers and panties exposing her bare bottom and legs. Austerley gasped, and Kirkgordon, as much as he had been thinking about this sight before, was unprepared for this sudden action. As Sam was about to step out of her knickers, Kirkgordon asked her to stop.

Austerley was quickly over to her. He reached out with his hand and felt her leg. There were scales appearing. Delicate, seemingly smooth and quite attractive, Kirkgordon thought, but definitely some form of scales.

As Austerley touched Sam's leg, she spun around and slapped his face. "Pervert!"

"But you are the one stripping off," said Austerley, looking at Kirkgordon to make a defence for him. "And besides I love those legs."

There was another slap.

"Easy, everyone. Sam, turn back around, we will too and get dressed, please."

"No, I want to swim, Kirky. I want to feel the water on my skin. That's where I should be, in the water."

"Okay," said Kirkgordon, now with his back to Sam hoping Austerley would follow his lead. "I understand this urge but maybe not so naked. I mean, where are you going to stop?"

"I don't know," said Sam, a tremor now in her voice. "I just know I want to feel the water on my skin. And these...scales, where did they come from?"

Kirkgordon heard the pain in her voice and turned around to see her start to sob. He delicately pulled her underwear back up to cover her, followed by her trousers before wrapping her up in a gentle hug.

"What is this? Tell me Kirky, what is this?"

"Transcendental tissue assimilation," said Austerley.

"Thanks, Indy, thanks. That helps no end."

Austerley shook his head. "Well it is, and it's quite beautiful."

"Will it come off?" asked Sam.

"Who knows?" answered Kirkgordon, "I've seen too much to know either way. All we can do is keep going. These sort of traps and defences will not stop Dr Howard, so we need to keep going. I'm sorry to have brought you into this. Sorry, that it's affecting you. But we need to keep going however it affects us." He held up his arm to her. "You never just walk away from this stuff. Physical are the more easily fixed wounds."

Sam nodded and held him again before stepping back. She dropped her trousers and sat down on the edge of the platform with her legs in the water. Kirkgordon joined her.

"That's better," said Sam. "Part of me wants to just take everything off and swim in the water. It's not erotic, it's totally a feeling, a desire to feel the water on my skin. It's like when you are cold and you are desperate to sit in front of a roaring fire. That's how I feel. Like I belong in the water."

Kirkgordon laughed. When he saw Sam begin to look hurt, he quickly spoke. "I'm not laughing at you, it's just that a part of me wants to see you take everything off and swim in the water. But it's definitely erotic!"

Sam punched his shoulder gently, and he saw her smile. As much as his statement was true, he was also keen to keep her mood up. *Who knows if we can ever get her back to normal? Still she looks good. Maybe I'm developing a thing for mutated women. No, it's just women, I'm like a retro Captain Kirk. Any race, any planet, any type of weirdness.*

"Time to go," said Sam slipping off into the water. Kirkgordon almost didn't wait for Austerley as he saw her enter the river.

28

The Grand Hall

Hannah landed solidly with both feet but then stepped forward with her left. The ground collapsed underneath that foot, and she desperately reared up, trying to lean backwards. But the movement was too much, and she could feel herself starting to fall forward. With her rear foot beginning to lift, she desperately pushed off as best as she could and flung her arms forward to help her jump further.

The ground beneath her body fell away as she landed on new markings. Her hands reached out scrabbling for anything as her body started to fall after the floor that had just given way. She could hear the pieces crashing down below her and felt her hands touch something solid and start to slide. And then an edge. She grasped hard with both hands.

At first the left didn't hold and she was swinging on just her right hand. Then she got her left hand onto something as her right slipped. With a strength borne in desperation, she managed to haul herself up and got both hands established on the edge, before pulling harder and placing the flat of her forearms on the surface. As she got over the edge, she looked but saw no markings on the floor. She had made it. She was on the other side.

There was a single pair of hands applauding her efforts. "Yes, you will certainly do. Right, guards stay here, the Doctor and I will be crossing over with our expendables. Make sure no one gets in here."

Hannah was still on the ground as the woman came across the path she had marked. Beside her was Dr Howard, still in his white suit and hat, looking rather nonplussed considering the power he was meant to be attaining. Instead, the woman was leading, strutting forward like a catwalk model, daring all with her glare. The expendables followed, clutching together as they walked the treacherous path across the large hall.

As they approached Hannah, the woman reached a hand down to help Hannah to her feet. The smooth skin looked almost waxy, and her eyes seemed to burn hypnotically as Hannah looked into her face. By contrast, Dr Howard walked right past, as if he hadn't seen her. The white trousers of his suit having soil marks up to mid shin, and his hat looked slightly cocked, giving a strange angle.

As she lifted Hannah to her feet, the woman seemed to be casting an inspecting glance, and then smiled wickedly as if indulging in the sight. "Time to go forward again, child. But take your sisters with you, for there is security in numbers. It's how most of the herd survive."

Hannah shivered at the laugh that followed but stepped on towards an archway that the woman pointed out.

*****

Havers was getting restless. The party had gone inside

some twenty minutes ago, and the guards were still watching the surrounding ground in diligent fashion. All he needed was someone not doing their job that well, just not watching well enough. As he scanned the posse of men defending the building, he thought he saw one, and on the edge too. Probably the most insecure position, and this man was being careless, casually glancing where a sentry's stare was required. *Good, very good.*

Havers moved away from the general area first, before deftly creeping back in from a different angle. Hidden by a large purple flower, he watched his man again, noting the cursory checking. The man was well over six foot with muscles aplenty, but he looked heavy on his feet. Speed was the key. Havers waited until the guard had moved to the edge of the party. Then, after the guard had started to turn back, he ran quickly and soundlessly. Being light on your feet was a skill acquired over years of practice, and Havers was among the best.

The neck was broken quickly from behind, and Havers had the small handgun removed just after the body hit the ground. Quickly checking the man's pockets, he removed a flashbang, a grenade and, most important of the finds, a silencer. There was also further ammunition for the weapon, an extra clip. He had counted eighteen guards in total. It should be enough, but his vantage point to begin was crucial.

Havers heard footsteps coming his way and dived for cover behind a yellow stem, taller and wider than himself. The fauna may have been strange, but it provided great cover. Another guard was approaching and was just coming across his fallen colleague when the double shot to the head took him down. Impassive, Havers searched the body and pocketed another clip. He spotted the radio on the body too. He would need to operate even quicker, before they were alerted.

Racing through the undergrowth, keeping foliage and plant between him and the guards in front of the building, he grabbed the flashbang and threw it back towards his tracks. Havers was well clear when the device sent out a blinding flash and a loud bang, all designed to disorientate in a small locale but now providing a distraction. Two guards ran towards the sound. Another grabbed his radio.

From the shelter of another purple flower, Havers picked off the radio operator first and then dropped both of the other responders as they turned on hearing him fall. He waited until a fresh party of three arrived and tossed his grenade at them. It exploded and sent the men falling this way and that, but it was also their last fall. Satisfied they were not going to stand up again, Havers ran quickly to a body and looted another flashbang and two grenades.

Without stopping, he again disappeared into the undergrowth and sought his next targets. With alacrity and guile, he tore his way through the men, dispassionately and brutally. Within three minutes, Havers stood alone at the entrance to the building. But now was his challenge, for these were mere guards, nothing to what lay ahead. Hannah needed him, and he was entering a lion's den, a place which rose from the sea and no doubt had powers beyond his knowledge. These things never ended well.

*****

The new hall that Hannah entered was vast. At the far end there was a great stone carving of what must have been Neptune or some similar god, Hannah believed. There was a trident and seaweed around the hand holding it, which seemed to be cut from some sort of clay that was still moist, like a wet putty from this distance. Before the carving there was a slab about the height of an average person's waist and several stools. Beyond that, there was an ornate seat, obviously detailed but from this distance the markings on it were unclear.

Before this area at the rear of the hall were various paths across from the generous flat ground after the arch. There appeared to be some sort of pool beneath these paths, and Hannah wondered at their nature. She scanned the room looking for some sort of clue and saw on the wall beside the arch what could be some sort of advice. Or maybe it was a warning. Although she couldn't tell the language, it seemed to be instructions rather than something ornate.

"Read it child, for you and your sisters will walk the paths for me, show me the right one to cross to the hallowed ground where we shall pay our respects to this power from beyond. Read child, for you will travel very soon."

Hannah watched the woman laugh and turned quickly to the markings on the wall. *I don't know this language but there must be something I can see. How many paths are there? Ten I can see. Is there any sort of list? Nothing dropping down like we would have them but then maybe they don't read like we do.* Hannah was beginning to panic. *Calm, come on and think, girl. You need this, you need it. Something with ten sections, ten somethings. Any repetition of that sort.*

It's there. Reading from the bottom and then right to left. It's like a table without the lines. There's something right there. Move across, those two have the same symbols, and those two are a pair, all the others seem to be of similar length except for that one. It's short. That one then. How do they number them? It's reading bottom and right. It must be number four. Number four. If I'm reading it right.

"Time to choose, child. And your sisters too. But you go first child, for I want to see you succeed. Lead me to the place of power." The woman indicated for Hannah to move. She thought about saying no. Thought about just running back. "I have ways to make you move," said the woman and Hannah watched her hand form a symbol in the air and a snake started to appear around her body. "I can let it come for you if you want, child. Walk to your place, all of you walk to the paths."

Hannah moved quickly to the path she saw as number four. It was damp and clay-like as if it had just formed from the potter's wheel. Stepping onto the beginning of her path, she saw beside it water, moving like a sea under swell. Her path rose up, but others moved up and down before they got to the other side.

For a moment Hannah felt guilty. If she had chosen right then these other women were to head to their doom, of whatever sort this mad place was bringing up. And they had no choice. She could have chosen differently and then they would have survived. *But Arthur wouldn't see that. We need to stop the Doctor from his plans, so I need to be alive. I don't see anyone else capable. If indeed I am capable.*

"Walk! Walk now to your future, walk and show me the path to power." The women looked at each other as if seeing who would move first. An older woman seemed to take it on board that she would go first and edged her way along the path before her. It took some minutes before she had ventured a quarter of the way across but then the water erupted. From below her path two large sides of a mouth erupted, either side of the path, sharp white teeth obvious on the gums. The mouth closed quickly over her and took the path she was standing on too, as it fell back to the water and was gone.

194

There was shrieking and wailing from the women. Hannah stood like stone, staring as water from the eruption drenched her. *Dear God, that was horrific, that was...* Even her thoughts stopped as the moment played back in her mind.

"So now we know more," laughed the woman who named herself after Death. "Who is next to walk? You on the far side, I think it is you."

The middle aged lady in a gown shook her head at the woman's remark. From around the woman's body a snake of at least ten metres emerged and slithered its way onto the path. The woman shrieked and turned and fled along the path. With her head looking behind her as the snake pursued, she didn't see the crumbling of the path ahead as she ran headlong into the collapsed section. Disappearing into the water, the lady gave no cry and there followed an eerie silence.

"One less! But I cannot wait to see if my chosen one has chosen well. So now you will walk, my child, for I bore of this game. Walk now and lead me to destiny."

Hannah gulped as the woman pointed at her. With a stuttering step, she moved forward. The way ahead looked alright, but the replay of the last few minutes was in her mind. With reluctant feet, she forced herself forward.

And then came a loud bang that followed a bright light from behind her. Turning around, Hannah saw her cousin, racing in through the arch. He quickly scanned this way and that before raising a hand gun and shooting the man in the white suit, Dr Howard. As the Doctor fell to the floor, Hannah screamed out to shoot the woman. But it was too late, and she had reacted. Hannah watched two ghostly snakes fly from her hands and bite into her cousin's shoulders causing him to promptly fall to the ground.

29

Scrolling

Kirkgordon was swimming strongly but he still marvelled at the woman ahead of him. It wasn't that he didn't enjoy her shape, but her effortless way of passing through the water was breath-taking. But, yes, the figure was extremely nice from behind too. His only regret was having to keep calling her back as they waited for Austerley to catch up as he floated along. Being water tight, Austerley's hollow leg had a buoyancy that caused him to tip backwards and look like the sedatest swimmer in history. It also meant he didn't go anywhere fast.

Calling out to Sam to hold up, Kirkgordon watched Austerley drift along. Two arms enveloped Kirkgordon from behind.

"You have a way of making people feel safer, do you know that?"

Kirkgordon wondered what had brought this on, and he turned in her grasp to face Sam. "It's only a feeling. People who follow me into places often don't make it back in one piece, if they make it back at all." *Father Jonah, Havers, Austerley, Calandra, Wilson and Alana.* The name struck him and he glanced down keeping clear of Sam's eyes.

"What is it?"

"My wife, she was one of the injured ones."

"Yes, you said. Is there something still there for her?"

"Sam, there's a whole heap of something in me for her. But she's changed, totally. She threw me across the room. And there's another space for Cally, the one who invaded Alana's patch. And now…"

"What?" asked Sam.

"And now you. It might just be the break from everything else, it might just be your easiness and a touch of affection I haven't felt in a while. But you are invading too."

"Is that alright?" Sam asked lifting his face up to hers.

"I don't really know. But don't stop. I think I need the company. Yeah, at the very least I need the company."

She nodded and kissed him on the forehead as Austerley passed by in the water. "Don't mind me. Or the rather important mission we're on with no idea how to solve."

"We'd get a room but the last one wasn't very cosy," laughed Sam.

And that's it. She's so easy to be around. It was always intense with Calandra, with Alana there was so much life in the way. With Sam, it's so easy, so chilled. And I don't know how or why. She's not even my type, since when did I like a blonde?

Sam swam off, passing Austerley, but remained in sight in the dark water tunnel. Kirkgordon had stressed to her the importance of maintaining sight of each other at all times. A wrong turn in this place, and they may never see each other again.

Soon Sam was swimming back towards him. She stopped occasionally, indicating some sort of blockage. *Great, we're going to have to get Austerley under the water.* Tagging along side Sam, he swam right up to where there was only wall. But the water was forcing him downwards and he was kicking hard to maintain the surface. Sam placed her arms around him and he didn't have to kick. It was like she was maintaining her spot without thinking and with a minimum amount of motion.

"Did you swim back at home?" he asked.

"A little, but it feels so much easier here, like I'm born to it."

And you are, thought Kirkgordon, *to the point of holding everyone else up.* Austerley arrived like a wayward li-lo, and Sam placed a hand on him, steadying him in the water. He glanced all around before pointing down.

"Yes," said Sam, "we'll have to go down. Should I search it out?"

"No, I'll go," answered Kirkgordon.

"Why? She should go, she's the best swimmer here."

Kirkgordon found himself agreeing with Austerley and knew something must be wrong. "I'll go with Sam. If there's trouble, she's unarmed and not experienced in conflict."

"And I just sit here floating?"

"Well, yes. Suited to being on your arse anyway."

Sam laughed. "You two are unreal. Come on." And she dived straight down. Kirkgordon didn't wait around and swam hard following Sam's behind down into the deep water. He couldn't see as it got deeper and a hand took his arm, steering him along a level before encouraging him to kick up and surface.

His head broke the water in a tunnel similar to that which he had left. But on one side there was a platform and an opening. He pointed it out to Sam, who nodded when he indicated she should stay in the water. With an effort he pulled himself onto the side. Cautiously, he edged up to the opening and then juked his head inside. He saw nothing threatening, so this time he let his head linger.

There were a number of scrolls on shelves, a desk of sorts to use although it was incredibly low. And there were tiaras and crowns. But they looked strange, as if designed for heads of varying shapes and sizes. Stepping into the room, he confirmed no one was there. He leaned back out of the room and indicated with a wave that Sam should join him.

Taken aback, as she leaped out of the water like a penguin, his eyes were honed on her legs, and she giggled as he realised she was watching his study of them.

"Proper workroom," said Kirkgordon, trying to sound serious.

"Hey, they are my legs, and you are free to stare. Just don't lose your edge watching me and miss the bad things out there. Oh, look, a table." Sam laid down at the low table, producing a slight curve that allowed her head to be just above the fixture.

"Why did you lie down like that? That's not normal."

"Well it feels normal. In fact, it feels perfect."

Kirkgordon reached out for a scroll and on opening it realised he had no clue about anything on it. *I need Austerley. He might understand some of this.*

"Sam, I need you to bring Austerley through to here. He might be able to read some of this." She nodded but walked towards him. A leg was curled around him and she pulled him close, not just with her arms but with everything. He felt her push and part his lips delivering a long and deep kiss and then her arms roamed his chest and buttocks.

He wasn't sure about responding. He wanted to, so much. But he knew his feelings were deep and he didn't want to cheapen any advance by disappearing in a few days. So he held back, merely holding her tight.

Sam stepped away. "That's where I want to be," she said. "Whenever, I'm ready."

He nodded. "I'm not yet."

"I know. I wish you weren't so decent as to not want to hurt me with something quick and meaningless. She was a lucky woman."

"Which one?"

Sam smiled. "All of them." Diving backwards, she entered the water like an Olympic diver, hardly a splash being made.

The least she could have done was be totally clueless about my motives. Or be annoyed. Or told me just to have fun, and we'd leave it behind. A flippant few nights on the cruise would have been easy. Who am I kidding, I don't do easy. It's all in or nothing. Even if my heart drags me in when my head says no.

Kirkgordon looked further around the room but found himself overwhelmed by the language displayed in front of him. It was a great weakness that he could only speak English, even French had eluded him at school. If there was a side to all this that escaped him, it was the whole culture of these things he investigated. *And that's why I'm still sane.*

A wet Austerley splashed onto the edge of platform outside and Kirkgordon helped him onto it fully. Sam then simply jumped out of the water beside him, smiling. *She is a distraction; I do need to keep my focus.* Turning to Austerley, he tried to get back on mission.

"I can't fathom any of this, Indy, I don't get this language at all."

"Languages. And of course you don't," said Austerley, picking up a nearby scroll and studying. "This is unusual. I've seen this language."

200

"Can you read it?" asked Kirkgordon.

"No. I said I had seen it. Trying to think where. The library in the Swiss Alps. Where we saw Scarlett. It had a copy of an old council decision paper brought back by someone who had crossed over. There was nothing else to cross-reference with it and so the paper was useless for translation, but that is, or is at least very similar to, that language."

"So what part of the world was it from?" asked Sam.

Austerley raised his eyebrows. "Not this one. Otherwise unknown. The person that crossed over was a bit of an ignoramus, otherwise they would have brought back a lot more."

The words "pompous ass" could be heard under someone's breath. Austerley grabbed another scroll. And then quickly another. And another. Then he stopped.

"What? What is it?" asked Kirkgordon.

"Shut up."

Sam looked over at Kirkgordon who shook his head in reply. Motioning for Sam to follow him, he exited the room.

He sat down on the platform, his legs dipped into the water. He was so wet it was hardly worth attempting to stay dry. In a seamless motion, Sam slid down beside him, her hand resting on his thigh.

"Listen Sam," he started, "I think we're going to have to continue on and follow this river or whatever it is further. Can you swim further up and see what's coming? Don't take any risks, you're just having a look. If there's any danger, any trouble, come straight back."

"Okay, just have a look." She seemed nervous.

"I'd come with you but…, you'd be quicker on your own. This skin, this thing that's giving you sleekness in the water,

201

you might have to own, even indulge it for a while, just to get back home safe."

"It's weird because part of me is drawn to it, loves it. But it's also not me, and that scares me. You two are used to this strangeness but back in the real world what would I do with it. People would run if I jumped out of the swimming pool like I do on this platform. I'd be a freak."

"Yes, you would. Some of us hide the freakishness," said Kirkgordon, holding up his arm for observation, and some have to wear it on their skin. And some like Austerley, they just ooze it. But if you can't get rid of it, you have to own it."

Sam took Kirkgordon's hand and placed it on her thigh, making him feel the strangeness of her skin which seemed to be becoming slippery. And then she lifted it up to her cheek, making his hand rub it until he moved his hand further back and took her hair in his hand whilst staring into her eyes.

She hides the fear well. But it's there in the eyes, that knowing that things have changed and wondering can they go back. Maybe that's part of the attraction, that she thinks I can deal with the strangeness. But she came on to me first back on the ship. Oh for the days of normal when I charged around the Middle East just protecting rich men and their women. The days of look but don't touch.

"Go," he said, "And be careful."

He watched her slip into the water, and the blonde hair fanned briefly before she submerged further. As he turned back to the room, he heard the surface of the water break and she called out.

"Hold these for me until I get back." Her head was above the water line and in her hands were a number of clothes. She threw them at him and smiled, before diving into the water. They landed on the platform but he saw her top and bra. Smiling to himself, he also cursed this was all happening here. Then her head broke through the water again. He indicated the clothes to her with his eyes.

"What? I'm owning it."

And owning me too. Stay safe, girl.

30

Part of the Place

When he heard the splash of her leaping out of the water, he tried not to look and stay focused on the scrolls and languages in the small room. Kirkgordon wondered that if Austerley hadn't been there would he have succeeded. *Of course not.* Walking out to the platform, he saw Sam pulling down her top.

"That felt great. It's like I just merge with the water. Like I belong with it."

Like that makes it all so much easier. What do I say? That's excellent Sam, get your kit off and dive back in?

"Did you see anything?" asked Kirkgordon, trying to focus on the matter in hand.

"Yes, but I had to be careful. I got through under the tunnel that's just beyond this and when I surfaced I could hear a lot of commotion. So I just stayed close to the opening I was in and listened at first.

"There was a woman's voice, speaking in a crazy fashion, like she owned the place, kept calling someone, *child*. I heard your friend too. She seemed to be taking orders, was quite

204

weepy. Occasionally there were a few others but not many."

"Did you hear the Doctor?"

"No, and I got curious so I decided to sneak a look. You might not believe this, but I can swim right up, almost past my knee out of the water and still hold my position, upright out of the water. It's crazy. And what with the speed I can swim at."

Kirkgordon could see Sam was struggling to remain on task. "Hold it. What did you see?"

"Oh, right. Well I came up just across from the Doctor. He seemed to be dead. Was just lying on the floor. But there was the dark skinned woman, and she's absolutely stunning close up, I tell you, amazing. She looks very hot in her outfit and…"

"Sam, she might be about to end the world, or at least enslave everyone as zombies, so can we focus here?"

Sam smiled. "Sorry, this is all new to me. It seemed horrifying at first but since this change has happened, it all starts to be more…fun. That sounds really lame."

"Exhilarating, you feel pumped up, like you've been charged at the main source of life, and although there's a churning in your stomach, you're almost born to it and are desperate to get back into the fray."

Sam looked at him with appreciative eyes. "You always feel like this? This is what you've been doing all these years and this is how you've felt?"

"Mostly, but it takes a toll. And not just on yourself." There was a moment of silence. "But go on, but without the bodily assessments of any women. I kind of get distracted by women, if you didn't realise."

Sam almost blushed. "Well, Hannah walked over a bridge type thing, of which there were quite a number. They all crossed from one side to the other of the room. I'm not sure there was any other way across. Also a couple of the bridges seemed to have been destroyed."

"And the woman."

"I'm coming to that. She followed Hannah over and there was the sound of something being dragged. I was able to do the swim thing where I raise right up. I saw a man being dragged by what seemed to be snakes of a type. But they were like the ghosts of snakes." At this Sam seemed to dwell, and Kirkgordon swore he saw her shiver.

"But the man, what did he look like?"

"I only caught a glance at his face, but you know what, he reminded me of Hannah."

"It's Havers. Shit, she's got Havers. At least he took out the Doctor. What did they do after that?"

"Well, I didn't hang around for too long, you said I was to stay safe. But they were on the far side of the hall. But I saw a big statue of that sea god from the films, you know Sinbad and Jason and that, the old ones with the monsters all shot by stop motion. Harry somebody did the monsters. But this was the guy that comes out of the sea."

"Poseidon, Neptune. What else?" asked Austerley, who had just emerged from the room behind.

"There was a big table and a chair, but the chair was really stylish, lots of glam and glitz, but in an old style way."

"Humph," muttered Austerley and wandered back into the room.

"What did I say?" asked Sam.

"He's busy trying to figure out what's happening. Don't worry, he goes like this. But he's good, if there's anything in there that will tell us what's occurring, Austerley will get it.

But you did good, Sam, real good." Kirkgordon turned back to the room.

"Kirky." He turned back and felt a kiss to his lips. "I feel something else. Like I'm meant to be here. Like I'm meant to stop that woman doing something. I can't explain it, except, this feels like home."

She walked past him into the room, and Kirkgordon felt something was wrong in what she had said. Even her legs going past couldn't distract him from this feeling, this thought that all was not right. What had the bite done to her really? It wasn't normal just to walk away from these things that happened without a cost.

Following her into the room, he saw Austerley in a whirl-wind of scrolls. He was picking up this one and then that one, before tossing them into the air. Then he would walk to the markings on the wall before grabbing more scrolls. Sam was looking at Kirkgordon, rather alarmed at this behaviour. He motioned for her to join him again on the platform.

Sitting down he placed his feet in the water, knowing she'd like this. Sure enough, she sat down beside him and began to let the water wash over her shins.

"He's just going through stuff. Every time he gets worked up or he'll go into a mood or something."

"Shouldn't we help him?"

"I doubt you'll know any of those languages. Austerley didn't seem to know them all, in fact, I'm not sure he knew any that well. And some of it seemed to be the native stuff, like we saw on the walls of the tunnels up to here. So I doubt we'd be of use."

Sam nodded. "I didn't realise then, but those were warnings. About the spears, about the water running down at us. Directions and that. I can't remember all the markings, but the room with the creature was telling the natives not to fear it, I think."

"And you just worked that out?"

"No, it's been coming to me ever since that creature bit me. I don't know why, but it's like I started to know what they meant."

Kirkgordon pondered and then jumped to his feet. "This way, Sam." Without waiting for a reply, he tore into the room and grabbed several scrolls and turned back to an oncoming Sam.

"Leave those bloody scrolls alone. You haven't the mind to deal with them," cried Austerley.

Ignoring him, Kirkgordon unfurled a scroll in front of Sam. "Can you read that?"

Sam looked, intently studying it. "Err…, no."

Kirkgordon unfurled another one. Sam shook her head. And another. Another shake of the head. One more. Same result. Kirkgordon threw the rest down in disgust, his idea seemingly come to nothing.

But Sam reached down and picked up a scroll that was partially showing its contents. "This one is about a seat, or maybe a throne, and some sort of power swapping."

Racing back to her, Kirkgordon snatched the scroll off her and turned and held it up in front of Austerley. "Is she right? Indy, is she right?"

"How should I know? That's the damn language of this place, I haven't a hope of cracking that with no context."

Kirkgordon suddenly saw what was happening. "You're becoming part of the place. It's no wonder you want to protect it. You're becoming something from here." He looked at

208

Austerley, who simply nodded.

"Wow," said Sam, "No wonder I feel alive."

31

To the Rescue

"The scroll, read the whole damn scroll. Then tell Indy all about it. Now, Sam, do it now."

Sam looked at Kirkgordon, and he realised that he must have been somewhat perplexing, a mix of anxiety and wonder. He saw a solution to the current problems, but he also knew that when these things take over a part of you, there's always a price.

"Come here, sit down," urged Austerley as he placed himself on the floor. Kirkgordon watched Sam sedately sit beside Austerley and felt a pang of jealousy. Giving her up to the expert while he just stood there, awaiting enlightenment. He always seemed to be making the decisions, and yet he rarely ever knew the answers. And even when he did, as in now, he had to sit it out while the experts got on with it. Sam was one expert he wanted to sit down with.

Stepping back outside the room, he watched the water below the platform. *A seat, a throne. Well, the Doctor was after some sort of power, they always were. But how did it work here? Come on, Sam, give me something to go on.*

She was taking on the form of the place. Calandra had taken on the witch's curse, and now she was so cold, cold enough to have burnt him. Alana had been infected by Dagon and wanted so very little of him in her madness. And now Sam, just when they had been, well he didn't know exactly what they had been but, she was changing. *Would it take her away from me too?*

"We have a problem." It was Austerley in his usual melodramatic fashion.

"A problem? I kind of realised there was a problem."

"This place," said Austerley, "is a kind of gateway, reaching out from a central power, coming and bestowing power on an individual in their world. And then it disappears, leaving them dominant in that place. But also connected."

"Connected?"

"Yes, to a degree, a puppet."

"To what degree?"

"Heavily influenced. Like a person with two voices in the head, driving the actions together. If one can take the power given, they will control elements, water, fire, not so sure about air. However, certainly water. But there's also a sacrifice. Human sacrifice, it won't work without it. They'll be taking people from the ship."

"So we need to move?" asked Kirkgordon.

"Yes, but there's also another issue. You have to complete the sacrifice in time, or the whole place dives back into the ocean, or more accurately I suspect, to another dimension."

"How long do we have?"

Austerley shrugged. The Professor made his way back into the room, and Kirkgordon saw him start to read a scroll whilst Sam appeared on the platform.

"He's beginning to read the language. I barely translated half of it, and I don't think I was that accurate, but he started reading it. His mind is amazing."

"At times," said Kirkgordon.

"No need to be jealous, he's hardly my type."

"I don't think I was being…" Kirkgordon saw Sam's eyes tell him he was lying. And he was. "Are you okay? Any other changes?"

"I don't think so, but then it's all so natural. I still want to shed everything and swim."

Kirkgordon swallowed. "Can you just keep that to yourself?"

"Don't you think it's a good idea?"

"I think it's a great idea, and I'm struggling to keep my mind off that image. But we need to keep it to business until we sort out this mess."

Sam laughed and watched him blush. "Okay, but we have a swim date afterwards. Are we going?"

"Yes," said Kirkgordon, "soon as Austerley is ready. We need to know what we're facing next and how to stop it. He'll work it out. He always does."

Kirkgordon left Sam dipping her feet into the water and sought out Austerley. He was still reading the scrolls, intent on a number of them. "I need short and simple, how we stop them, Indy?"

"No sacrifice, no power, that's one absolute. We need to stop the sacrifice. And get off the island quick. When it goes down, it is quick. Like when it appeared. Just popped up right out of the ocean. And it'll go down the same."

"Okay, so raise hell and stop things happening and get out."

"Yes, but here may be another factor."

"What?"

"If I'm right on my internal clock, it might be getting dark outside soon. Vampires. They'll sense the power, and they'll be here. And you're a target, after disposing of one of theirs."

"Me?" said Kirkgordon. "What about you?"

"I've always been a target for many things they perceived that I have done."

"Perceived?"

"Yes. Perceived accurately, but nonetheless, perceived. Nothing proven."

"Alright, then come on, I think we need to be moving. From what Sam saw last time, we may be up against it. Are you ready?"

"Yes. I think I can tap into the power too. But it's an unknown."

"Okay. But take it carefully. Don't wipe us all out."

Kirkgordon called to Sam who came in and listened to Kirkgordon explaining how she would lead Austerley under the water to the large hall she had seen. They were to keep a low profile whilst a read on the situation was taken. And then they would strike and evacuate.

Austerley dropped unceremoniously into the water, while Kirkgordon dived in. Sam somersaulted in, entering without as much as a splash. Grabbing Austerley's hand, she led the way through the underwater tunnel and brought them up slowly into the great hall she had seen.

Peering as much as he dared above the path by the water, Kirkgordon saw the dark skinned woman with Hannah on the far side of the hall. She was standing next to a large slab or table and there was a throne nearby. The great clay carving of Poseidon dominated the hall and seemed to be glowing somewhat.

"Havers is on the slab," said Kirkgordon in a hushed whisper, "Some sort of snakes or something with him. The woman is over him, and she appears to have a few others with her. Women, looking like zombies. Hannah is over at the throne."

"Is that it?" asked Austerley.

"We'll have to get close up if we're going to get a chance to get her."

"Careful," warned Austerley, "she's powerful. We'll need to be quick."

Kirkgordon nodded and gently submerged back underwater. He felt Sam swim past him, and he followed her path. Cautiously, he broke the surface after her. There was a chant now ringing around the air and lifting himself to the lip of the walkway he was beside, Kirkgordon saw a host of women, voices raised but eyes glazed over. One of them was taking a large knife from the dark skinned woman, who was giving instructions on how to butcher Havers.

There was no sign of Doctor Howard's body and the elimination of Havers seemed imminent. There was no time to get Austerley caught up. The dark skinned woman turned and walked to the throne and began to chant out something unknown to Kirkgordon.

The water began to bubble and what had been the serene calm of the pool was now a riotous mess as jets of water flew into the air. The woman who held the knife, still looking like a zombie, held it up over Havers. Kirkgordon pulled himself up and into view of everyone. The woman held the knife over Havers and was about to plunge.

The arm had flown open and about to deliver a bolt to the poor woman when a blur shot past his eyes. He then saw Sam spring out of the water and clatter to the ground.

"You, what gives you the right to deny me my power?" The dark skinned woman stood up. "I am evil, I am here to take your soul." She let something out of her hand and a shape hit Kirkgordon in the chest, taking him over the side and into the pool.

Austerley emerged from the water behind Kirkgordon and reached out with his arms, and presumably his mind, towards Havers, forcing the woman to release him and focus on the Professor. Hannah ran towards her cousin but was thrown back towards the wall.

"No, this power is mine, all mine and you shall all fall!"

"I think you forgot our invite," said a hollow voice. It spoke of cold and cruelty, and its owner stood wrapped in a black cape looking extremely theatrical. "But you seem to have brought plenty to feast on."

Kirkgordon was struggling in the water and had to duck as a shadow passed over head. Austerley wasn't as lucky as he was picked up by the shoulders. "Good evening, Professor, we have waited a long time for you."

Then a shot rang out as the vampire carrying Austerley was sent spinning, and Austerley fell into the water. Kirkgordon tracked it to a man with a special tattoo on the side. "Oh hell, not these vigilantes too. Sam, Sam where are you?"

Kirkgordon tried to work out if more of the tattooed people were here. But as he reached around he caught a dark shape beneath him gradually getting bigger. He swam like fury but was launched up and up, into the air. This was crazy, how did you fight on this basis? As he reached the apex of his flight, he realised that the thing that had flung him up was also now readying its mouth.

"Rope!" Kirkgordon felt the bolt find something solid, and

he stopped the rope coming out, swinging towards Sam who was now cornered. With a deft grab, he swung again with her now in his arms before letting her fall into the water. He continued on the swing himself and found the fist of a waiting vampire.

As he fell to the ground, he briefly saw Austerley engaged in arm waving again. And he looked towards the slab as he stood up. *Havers was gone. Havers was loose.* And a punch knocked him to the ground again.

32

Battle Royale

Kirkgordon winced as his jaw was hit a second time. The eyes that now filled his face were wild and there dripped blood from the jaws. But unless he had been sedated, it wasn't his blood. Desperately he turned his firing arm around towards that face and grinned when a bolt glanced off the head, spinning the vampire off him. He rolled away to the other side and tried to stand. But the vampire kicked him in the guts.

The wind was driven out of him, and he struggled to grab his breath. He felt a hand grab his hair but then it released again. He waited for more pain, but he seemed to be left alone. He rolled onto his back, seeing the vampire stood over him. The creature was over six feet tall and built like a muscle man. Even if it didn't have the superhuman strength attributed to this form of the undead, he would have been formidable.

"Delighted to meet your acquaintance, dear fellow. If you would kindly leave my colleague alone, I think we can come to an accommodation."

Havers. Thank God, it's Havers. Stalling to make a plan,

sounding like a posh arse but actually buying time and formulating. It'll be time to get up soon.

From his prone position, Kirkgordon watched the vampire step over him and run, arms outstretched, towards Havers. The consummate professional, Havers dodged to one side before coming up behind the vampire and grabbing its neck in a lock from behind. There was a snap and Havers let the creature drop to the ground.

"Shoot the neck now!"

Kirkgordon did as instructed but didn't relish the sight of the head detaching from the body. But it was necessary. There was no wood, no holy water, nothing else to pin them down.

"Good man, Mr Kirkgordon, I feel somewhat outgunned with so many parties involved."

"Austerley says that the place will sink again if there's no sacrifice. We need to stop any sacrifice on that slab. And then get the hell out when this place goes into reverse."

Havers nodded. "Then we need to get to the slab, clear everyone away and defend it. If one gets caught up in individual brawls, someone will get through."

Kirkgordon looked to the slab and saw Austerley engaged in battle with the dark skinned woman. She was manipulating a number of ghostly snakes in his direction which he was currently stopping with a wall of fire he had conjured from somewhere.

Firing a rope bolt into the ceiling, Kirkgordon offered a hand to Havers. There was a shake of the head and so Kirkgordon lifted his feet and began to swing across the water dividing him from Austerley. As he lifted he felt two hands grab his shoulders and Havers was on his back.

Swinging across the water, Kirkgordon spotted a man on

one of the paths below. He seemed to be from the secret organisation who had been protecting this place. Havers slid off his back and clattered into the man from a height. Seeing the man roll and come back up on Havers, Kirkgordon feared for his colleague. But Havers swung his feet from his low position, upending the man, before striking the jaw.

Turning back to his own destination, Kirkgordon let the rope go loose as he landed behind Austerley.

"Have you got this?" shouted Kirkgordon.

"You idiot, she's too powerful, she's tapped into this place."

"So why don't you?"

"Because it's a controlling force. It's keeping her here. She thinks it'll let her go, she will be greater than it, but it won't." The flames suddenly stopped. "Shit, hit her with something."

"Flame!" shouted Kirkgordon. He fired off three bolts in front of the woman and a sudden blaze went up. But she remained impassive and instead turned to one of the group of woman she had brought in with her. The dark haired subject became glazed over and grabbed Hannah by the arm. Another hostage joined her and Hannah was dragged to the slab.

She yelled. There was nothing she could do as they dragged her to the slab. Meanwhile the dark skinned woman started walking towards Kirkgordon and shot ghostly snakes from her hands that slithered towards him. He back tracked but was soon at the water's edge.

"Mr Kirkgordon, you have this. Understand me, you have that situation."

What the hell is he on about? I'm kind of outgunned here. Totally outgunned. I'm firing bolts and they are disappearing through the ghosts. What am I meant to do? Distraction, he's distracting. Draw her away.

Kirkgordon ran along the path's edge firing off bolts towards the woman but the snakes were catching up. They formed a pincer movement, and he was suddenly trapped, one from either side. Firing a rope bolt to the ceiling, he was dismayed when the ceiling began to crumble. *Is that the island starting to go back down?* But there was no time for contemplation as the snakes approached. There was only the water behind, but he remembered the creature who had thrown him to the air.

With no choice, he fell backwards. The water offered no resistance and he tried to swim down, believing the snakes may follow. Then from beneath he saw the large shadow moving quickly up towards him. This time the mouth seemed open.

Then a blur passed in front, and he felt arms wrap around him. He was raced to the surface and up into the air. His eyes saw Sam's face before him but she was deep in concentration and then he was caught unawares as they crashed into more water. And then suddenly they were back in the air, and she was letting him go. He landed on the floor and slid into a clay wall.

A pair of wet legs landed before him.

"Are you alright? Sorry, overdid that."

His head was sore, his shoulder complaining but his eyes thought this might be the place to stay. But there was no time.

"Sam, come on. Take me to the slab." He stood up and ran back to the water, taking Sam by the hand. As they fell into the water, he felt her wrap herself around him again. The journey in the water was short but at an incredible speed. *What was she becoming?*

They cleared the water and this time landed more gently. For a moment he looked at her, drew in his breath before turning away towards the slab. It was empty but surrounded by Austerley, Havers and Hannah. The dark skinned woman stood on one side whilst the other had a small posse of vampires including the one Austerley had described as the potential queen.

"Step aside," said the queen, "and you can walk away. I'm a reasonable person. We'll sacrifice her and then that'll be another of your problems sorted." She was pointing at the dark skinned woman, who was looking more sullen than before.

"Walk away for how long? This power does not need to be in this world," cried Austerley. "It doesn't seek to share, it will twist whatever you have into its will. It's tainted. Completely tainted."

"It's mine. It wants me. And I shall have it!" cried the dark skinned woman.

The queen motioned one of her subjects, and a vampire flew at the woman. She raised a hand and a ghostly snake raced out opening a large fanged mouth very wide. The vampire flew straight into the mouth and began to shudder. Then it suddenly crumbled into dust.

"Vladimir. No!" the queen cried. Again she signalled and this time the remaining vampires launched themselves over the slab at the woman. Kirkgordon noticed that the Poseidon figure on the wall was glowing strongly and crack lines were forming around its edges.

"Austerley, what is that?" asked Kirkgordon.

"It's coming. Coming to take us back," said Sam, "You should go."

The sound of the vampires suddenly crumbling, snapped Kirkgordon's view back to the slab. The queen was now panicking, and Austerley seemed to be deep in thought. Then a piece of clay wall fell beside Kirkgordon.

The shock caused him to turn and he saw Sam beginning to shake.

"What's happening?" he asked her.

"It's coming. Coming to take us all. Coming for the queen."

Austerley half limped as fast as he could to Kirkgordon and Sam. He was sweating, but the sweat was cold. He looked at Sam and then the wall. A sudden thud caused everyone to look at the queen who was thrown against the wall. She was then dragged by something towards the water. As she was about to enter the water, a swirl rose to meet her.

"Something's coming for her. Look at the tattooed people, they are fleeing," shouted Austerley.

Kirkgordon saw the remaining tattooed people, on the far side of the water, turning and running for the exit from the hall. He looked at Austerley. "What's it going to do? Just grab her and go? What?" Austerley shrugged.

"It's coming to go back. I feel it," said Sam. "Like going home. I feel like I'm going home."

"We need to go," yelled Kirkgordon. "We don't want to get dragged down with it."

"Follow me," shouted Havers, "Hannah knows the right path back."

Kirkgordon watched Havers, Hannah and Austerley race past him and indicated for Sam to go. But she shook her head.

"This is home coming. Kirky, this is what I am that's coming. I can't go, it's calling me."

Kirkgordon didn't have time to argue. But could he knock her out and carry her? Could he convince her with the right words? Despite having only known her a few days, something inside didn't want her to leave, something felt she was closer than she should be.

222

"I'm your home, Sam. I'm your home." And he grabbed her and kissed her deeply. He felt her respond. Willingly and freely and with a gusto that invigorated him.

And the building shook. It was seemingly having a tantrum at the petulant child who had just gone to a stranger. *Oh hell,* thought Kirkgordon, *it still wants her.*

"Run, Sam, run!"

33

Back to the Sea

"Which path?" shouted Kirkgordon.

"That one," chorused Sam and Hannah together.

How could Sam know that? She's a part of the place, a part of it.
Kirkgordon took the lead along the path followed by the rest of his motley crew. Although it rose slightly to clear the water, the path was reasonably smooth, if somewhat wet after all the splashing from the water. They were about halfway across the bridge when Kirkgordon saw something in the water. A dark shape he recognised too well.

The path before him shattered as a dark blue creature tore up through it, white teeth evident. As the creature fell back down, Kirkgordon fired off several bolts at it before deciding on another course.

"Hannah, Havers, with me." The pair stepped forward as Kirkgordon launched a rope bolt into the ceiling. As he tugged the rope to make sure it was sturdy, he saw bits of clay flake close to it. *Ah well, no time to make sure.* He grabbed Hannah by the waist and allowed Havers to jump onto his shoulders.

With a small run up, he started into a swing that took them across open water, his eyes scanning for a blue shape coming up from below.

But they landed safely on the other side, Kirkgordon depositing Hannah while Havers alighted. Kirkgordon continued the swing and made his way back across. As he was over the original site of his departure, the rope gave way from the ceiling, and he crashed onto the ground. Sam was over in an instant and began to haul him up.

"I'll swim you over."

"I can't leave Austerley here. He's too precious, they can't have him. Swim Austerley over, I'll follow."

Sam looked anxious with the plan, but she did as she was asked and took Austerley's hand. Watching the pair fall into the water, Kirkgordon fired again into the ceiling. On catching into the clay, he pulled the rope to test it and a large chunk of ceiling fell off, causing him to back track before the dislodged piece crashed into the path, smashing it up again.

Kirkgordon turned and ran back towards the slab. As he approached, a stream of water shot out of the main pool, like a lasso approaching its victim. He dived behind the slab as the water hit it, sending the top flipping off into the rear wall where it shattered.

Further streams of water began to shoot out and he sought further shelter. There was none around and so he fired up into the ceiling again. When the bolt bit he didn't wait but instead made his rope retract sending him up into the air above the streams. However, halfway up he began to fall again as ceiling gave way. At this height he was unlikely to survive intact, so he fired an armour bolt at the ground when he was going to land. There was an explosion that caused dust to billow into the air.

At first it was choking and dry, before he fell through the gap he had created and crashed into the water below. His eyes were open but the water was dark, down beneath the platform, looking at the shades of blue around him he pointed himself to where he thought the open water was and began to swim. Inside his head, there were thoughts of something large and dark which would bare its teeth and then the fight would be over.

The strangest thing was sound in the water. Above him things were collapsing, clay was hitting water and foundations were shaking but below the surface everything was muted. Like a tape deck which had slowed down, there was a slur to everything that threatened to obliterate the correct impression. In all this confusion, swimming for his life as he was, he was finding a moment of calm in the storm when things outside of the danger were permeating his mind.

But then he saw the dark shape. It was still some way off but was moving quickly, filling up his view with a darker blue, coming out of the lighter shade of salvation. Instinctively he turned around to swim away but there was nothing that direction except the underside of the platform. No, this was it. Still the others had Havers to get them clear. It would be okay. His breath was almost gone, and he felt his limbs struggling to make an impact now on the water as the lungs emptied of useful air.

The embrace was strong. Wrapped up in a pair of arms, he felt his head nestle below her chin. Her skin felt good, something to go remembering. And then the water was rushing past him at a speed that defied belief. And then the open air and the thud of landing on the ground.

He gulped, desperately sucking in the oxygen surrounding him. For a moment, he was disorientated, lost in a panic for life, lungs processing as fast as they could. And then her face was before him. Smiling, but also wondering, concerned. He sat up and looked around. They were on the far side of the hall, away from the platform and close to an entrance to another hall.

"No time, Mr Kirkgordon, we need to go and this next bit is no easier. Kindly get to your feet, Hannah will need to lead us."

"Go, Havers, I'm good, I'm coming now." Kirkgordon took a hand offered by Sam and got to his feet. His head was swimming, but he forced himself to focus. Before him was a broken floor, a mesh of symbols and Hannah staring intently.

"I can't remember," she cried, "I can't remember."

"You have to, my dear, just focus, let it all slip away and just focus," advised Havers.

"Just focus. Bloody hell, Arthur, how? Tell me how?" The girl was shaking, and she looked ready to swoon.

"Listen to my voice, and remember. Listen carefully and think back to that moment when you first crossed. What symbols did...Mr Austerley, what the hell do you think you are doing?"

Austerley had stepped forward onto several symbols. "The language is quite easy once you have someone to give you a start. I'm no expert, not yet, but I think with something as basic as this I'll be ok." He stepped onto another symbol.

"Indy," said Kirkgordon, "take the rope and tie it around you." Kirkgordon had removed a rope bolt and tossed it to Austerley.

"I doubt we'll need that. As I said the language is quite easy."

227

"I insist. Just bloody do it."

"Okay," said Austerley tying it around him. "But you'll see there will be no need..."

The floor beneath Austerley crumbled, and he fell forward out of sight. Bracing for the pull of the rope, Kirkgordon was delighted to find Havers had stepped across and provided extra help with anchoring him.

"Hannah, Sam, help pull the stupid arse up." With the building shaking and pieces of ceiling and wall crumbling, the pair set to their task quickly and it was but a few moments before they had Austerley back up.

"That was the wrong symbol. It's very close to the other one. Need to look closer."

"Indy, on your feet but have Hannah and Sam over your shoulder. Make sure with them. But hurry. Soon this place is going to tumble down."

As if responding to Kirkgordon's cue, a large chunk fell out of the ceiling and destroyed the path across from them, pieces disappearing to the abyss below. The comical team of Austerley in his loud Hawaiian shirt, with Hannah and Sam flanking him on either side reminded Kirkgordon of that Millionaire with his Bunny girls. It was a disturbing thought as he saw Austerley grab the women around the shoulder from time to time to examine another piece of ground.

Progress, whilst not slow, wasn't overly quick. And something was kicking at Kirkgordon's mind. If the island was going down, then outside there might not be any land. There might be only water. Austerley was a rubbish swimmer, but at least Sam would be good to get him away. Hannah was an unknown and Havers? Well, Havers did everything well.

They reached the far side of the crumbling floor, and

Kirkgordon dropped the rope to Austerley. He strode down the steps of the building and it was as he had feared. The island had begun to sink and there were now only small patches of land above the water. A mix of sea and dark soil surrounded most of the ridiculously coloured plants and Kirkgordon wondered how best to manage this.

"Havers, take lead. Get us a path to the ship. Then you Hannah, Austerley, Sam, and I'll cover our rear. Careful, some patches of water will be deeper than others."

Havers set off splashing though the weird landscape, Hannah close behind and then Austerley, plodding awkwardly. Watching him, reminded Kirkgordon of a limping duck he had seen at a local park. Fortunately, Sam was close behind and when Austerley stumbled she would lean forward and support him, correcting him. Kirkgordon swore at times she wasn't standing on anything solid but she was able to take the weight put onto her.

The island was sinking further, and the water was rising to their knees by the time they reached the area near the ship. On the decks of the ship were a large number of people, no longer zombies but now shouting and pointing at the island and these five desperate souls. *Good, we may get help to get on board. And no zombies, so she must be dead.*

As they were close, Kirkgordon fired a rope bolt onto a clear deck of the ship. Feeling the line grip, he called to Havers to climb it. Hannah was ordered onto Havers back, and the pair looked like some circus act as he tore up the rope.

"Indy, get going. We haven't a lot of time for your hanging around and getting ready, this island could drop any minute. And I'll be the only one on the rope."

Austerley shot him a dark look but wrapped arms and legs

around the rope, beginning to shimmy up in an awkward fashion. Nodding to Sam to follow, he watched her step onto the rope and walk up it behind Austerley. As deep in a moment of haste and terror as he could be, his male mind still took on board the sight of her bottom wiggling as she walked up the rope. To distract himself, he checked Havers progress and saw him clear the barrier of the deck. Quickly, Havers turned around and urged the others on.

And then it happened. The island fell away from beneath him and the rope went slack causing Austerley to fall into the water. Around Kirkgordon a swirl was forming and Sam appeared by his side, seemingly struggling in the water for the first time he had ever seen. Austerley had disappeared and Kirkgordon was hanging on for his life.

"Get Austerley, Sam. I'll be okay, you get Austerley."

There was a look of fear, almost a moment of resignation before she dived. The whirlpool had grown stronger, and he could feel the force dragging at his legs. But he watched her blonde hair disappear beneath the waves longing to dive with her.

Several lifebelts hit the water near him. Desperately he grabbed one and felt the pull of it against the surge beneath him. He could see Havers coming down the line of the rope, taught as it had now become, shouting at him to hold on. But the pain was building.

"Go! Havers, go back. It's too strong. My shoulder's starting to give. Go back. They need you at HQ. There's a demon to deal with. Wilson won't be enough. Tell Ma'am, it's not black and white, we'll need all the grey we can muster. Tell her I said you need to lead."

Havers called for another rope to be flung to him and duly

230

caught it. "Why me, Mr Kirkgordon?"

"Because you're the hardest bastard I know." Kirkgordon smiled. "I'm going for Austerley. Tell Ma'am I'll be back. And tell my kids too."

"And I thought it was the woman you were going after."

Kirkgordon laughed crazily and then winced at the pain in his arm. "Scarlett O'Meara. Take Scarlett with you, stronger than she knows. Better looking than Austerley too." And with that he was gone, the rope cut from his bolt arm, falling backwards, arms outstretched into the surf.

Havers saluted and then climbed back up the rope.

34

Epilogue

Havers stared out to sea from the pool deck at the rear of the cruise vessel. Things had settled down and a lot of passengers were coming to terms with having been zombies. Some were coming to terms with what they had done whilst being in the trance state and some were simply being identified for the next of kin.

It's a damn mess, thought Havers, *a damn mess. And for what. Lost probably the greatest mind, strange and other worldly, and also the best man in just getting things done. It's not often I think of someone out performing me, but Mr Kirkgordon always got things done. Not elegantly, not perfectly, but always done. And he had this time, it was just that he had gone down with the ship.*

He heard Hannah approaching behind him, her steps echoing across the floor but they were tentative, hesitant and somewhat questioning. She had been shaken up by the whole experience, and he placed no blame on her for that. After all she was no field agent, more of a bookworm. In the days to come, with Mr Austerley now missing, he may need her more.

A hand was placed on his shoulder and he reached up with

his hand, holding hers.

"Are you okay, cousin?"

"No, Hannah, I am not okay. I've lost two of the best operatives I've ever worked with and apparently there's a demon on the loose. I could have done with Mr Austerley for that one. Still, I have you."

"And your hunt for Ohlos' killer?"

"Will have to wait. Ma'am needs me now."

"Well it's good to have you back again, Arthur. Hopefully you'll get a rest."

"I doubt it, Hannah. After all, it's for Queen and country we serve. I think I need to go and see her. But while we travel you can answer a few things for me. First off, who is Scarlett O'Meara?"

*****

His arms were in agony. Kirkgordon reckoned he had been hanging by them for at least four hours, and he wanted to touch the floor that was a mere two feet below. Then again that was the point when you were a prisoner, giving you the false hope. Austerley was missing. He hadn't seen him when he entered the water but had ended up landing on the island which had become dry again. His mind whirled around how that happened and where the whirlpool of water he had fallen into ended and the dry land had begun. But there was nothing coming to mind that made sense.

Sam was across from him, held down by shackles a few inches from a pool. It seemed to be torture for her not to be in the water. Almost like she was drying out. Her body had a sheen which had turned her skin an aquamarine colour, and the hairs you would have expected and other bodily features had seemed masked in some way so that while she was

233

naked, the erotic features were covered. Well, the small parts anyway, her cleavage was still substantial and Kirkgordon had struggled not to stare despite his situation.

One thing he was sure of was that he needed to escape. There had been a few other prisoners taken away and none had returned. Most had looked like they were off to their last event, and so he decided he had no time to wait and see the lay of the land.

The guards looked like Sam, in that their skin was the same but the humanoid figures seemed devoid of human characteristics, such as expression and had staring bulbous eyes. They also uttered a language Kirkgordon didn't recognise and seemed somewhat dull, functioning only in their duties and not looking for any further engagement. But they did carry the keys to the shackles.

It had been four hours and every time there was more than one of them. But now, one entered and walked over, on feet that almost were flippers, to the pool beside Sam. He splashed his arms in and threw water over himself. Then he dripped a handful on Sam and made a laugh of sorts. It had been the first form of solo expression Kirkgordon had seen and hope was kindled.

"Hey, fish man, come over here. I need your keys."

The creature looked over and obviously decided there had been an insult. Kirkgordon hung looking at death's door and the creature came close and began to swing its thick arm and webbed hand. Kirkgordon reared up suddenly, lifting his body high and then dropping his legs around the creature's head. With all his strength he twisted his legs until he heard a snap. Holding the creature in his legs, he lifted it up until the key chain was at his teeth. Then after taking hold of the chain, he dropped the creature, which then lay motionless on the ground.

With his mouth he worked the key into a position of use and lifted himself to his bonds. A few seconds later he had one hand free, and then he released himself fully dropping to the floor. His arms ached and he fought to put them by his side. Looking up he saw Sam, her eyes wide with hope.

"Let's go, it's time to go home. And we'll pick up that stupid arse on the way."

35

Bonus Prologue SETAA Book 2: Alana Kirkgordon, The Darkness Within

"**M**a'am, I would not suggest such a course of action if one's hands were not tied, but I fear that she is our best choice."

He watched the woman with the scarf tied around her head look down at the paperwork through her dominating glasses. Clearly she was conflicted by this option before her, but then so was he. Havers had taken two days to come to the conclusion that this was the card to play. Having returned from the Caribbean and the island that sunk into the sea taking two of his best operatives, he was without a leader and also without someone whose connection to the dark things of the world ran deep. He could compensate for the first but no one currently in the agency could replace Mr Austerley.

"And did you go to see her?" asked the woman before sipping a cup of tea.

"Yes, Ma'am. When I read the reports about the words she

had said, the images spoken of and answers and other matter given out, I realised it might be an opportunity. Her encounter with Dagon profoundly changed her, but we did not realise the extent until recently."

"If I might interject." Wilson paused until the woman in the scarf nodded. "It has profoundly affected her. She is violent, abusive, sometimes I believe she's looking to kill. There is no way we should introduce such an unstable asset into a potentially explosive situation. She might even be turned."

The woman turned her head and lifted her eyebrows at Havers.

"Yes, Major Wilson is correct with his analysis, but she is our only connection. You cannot defeat these beings without knowing what they are and without tapping into the power around them. She is a necessary evil in all this. An evil I will personally supervise."

The woman stood up and walked to the large range where a kettle sat. She took her cup and poured another round of tea, then indicated at the men if they wanted another. On refusal, she set the kettle down and turned to stare out the window.

"Mr Austerley, whilst erratic, was definitely much more stable than this woman. And he also had a protector."

"I shall protect her and others from her," countered Havers.

"Mr Kirkgordon did not provide only physical protection, he had a moral compass. With recent events, your wanderings in search of personal revenge, am I to trust you, Major Havers?"

"I understand your concerns, Ma'am, but the cloud before me over Ohlos' death is gone. We will catch up with Farthington when the time comes and not before. Besides, Ohlos would not have wanted me to go to the places I ended up in. But I am here, focused and ready."

"Ma'am," said Wilson, "You handed the agency to me because of concerns about Major Havers state of mind, and he has not completed any psychiatric reports, retraining or debriefing. I would move that it is unwise to involve him in this critical situation we face until such time as we are fully convinced of his stability."

Havers shot a look at Wilson and prepared to speak but the woman turned around and stood with both hands leaning on the table.

"Major Wilson, your concerns are noted and to a large degree, I concur. However, I do not believe we are in a situation to play anything safe with my best operatives lost to a disappearing island. With regard to this demon, Major Havers will head up the task force to determine this demon's plans purposes and send it back to where it came from.

"However, Major Wilson will retain overall charge of the agency and as such I am promoting you to a new rank to show the difference between a mission head and the operational head. Congratulations, Colonel Wilson. Major Havers, you will report through the Colonel to me.

"As for the poor woman, it seems to me we do not have the luxury to play it safe, so bring her onto the team, Major Havers. But rest assured, all her actions are your responsibility. And keep her safe and well, lest you incur the wrath of her husband."

"Yes, Ma'am." Havers smiled and made sure that Wilson knew it.

"Dismissed, gentlemen. Oh, and Major Havers, stay a moment." Wilson looked strangely at the woman, but he knew his place and retired from the room.

The woman sat down again and motioned for Havers to pull

a chair up close.

"I am glad to see you, Arthur, your fall was most distressing, but then again, I should never have doubted your ability to recover yourself. However, I am most annoyed at your lack of faith to the mission. Your anger nearly scuppered Mr Kirkgordon."

"My apologies Ma'am. Ohlos was dear to me. He saved my life on many an occasion."

"And he was dear to me as well. Understand that if you turn from the mission again, I will throw you out, never to work with the department again." Havers nodded. "And no petulance to the Colonel, he has performed terrifically in your absence. But I need someone special for this task. Someone who can get it done. And in the absence of Mr Kirkgordon, it will have to be you."

"I shall endeavour to not disappoint."

"Damn well don't, Arthur. And as for Mrs. Kirkgordon, bring her back safe and well."

Havers nodded. *Alana Kirkgordon, life is about to change again.*

About the Author

GR Jordan is a self-published author who finally decided at forty that in order to have an enjoyable lifestyle, his creative beast within would have to be unleashed. His books mirror that conflict in life where acts of decency contend with self-promotion, goodness stares in horror at evil and kindness blind-side us when we at our worst. Corrupting our world with his parade of wondrous and horrific characters, he highlights everyday tensions with fresh eyes whilst taking his methodical, intelligent mainstays on a roller-coaster ride of dilemmas, all the while suffering the banter of their provocative sidekicks.

A graduate of Loughborough University where he masquer-aded as a chemical engineer but ultimately played American football, Gary had worked at changing the shape of cereal flakes and pulled a pallet truck for a living. Watching vegeta-bles freeze at -40'C was another career highlight and he was also one of the Scottish Highlands "blind" air traffic controllers. These days he has graduated to answering a telephone to people in trouble before telephoning other people to sort it out.

Having flirted with most places in the UK, he is now based in the Isle of Lewis in Scotland where his free time is spent between raising a young family with his wife, writing, figuring out how to work a loom and caring for a small flock of chickens. Luckily his writing is influenced by his varied work and life experience as the chickens have not been the poetical inspiration he had hoped for!

You can connect with me on:
- http://www.grjordan.com
- http://www.twitter.com/carpetless
- http://www.facebook.com/carpetlessleprechaun
- https://www.amazon.com/G-R-Jordan/e/B00P6WP9FS

Subscribe to my newsletter:
- http://grjordan.com/download-footsteps

Also by G R Jordan

G R Jordan writes fantasy books in several series, including the Austerley & Kirkgordon series of which you have just read the fourth. At the time of publishing there are 3 origin stories and 4 full length novels. Published books from other series are detailed below, including the feel good fantasy series, Island Adventures.

Scarlett O'Meara: Beastmaster

Cursed with a talent she never knew. Bestowed a gift everyone wants. Scarlett must embrace her mother's legacy to stop a lecherous shadow preparing a demon's army.

"Scarlett O'Meara" is the first story in the urban fantasy maelstrom that is the SETAA series from the pen of G R Jordan. Featuring Calandra, the Ice Maiden from the well loved Austerley & Kirkgordon series, this tale introduces a buxom, feisty lass from the Welsh valleys to the strange powers that threaten to destroy our world. If you love plucky heroines, fantastic creatures and wild supernatural action, then you'll love these tales from Britain's most secret agency. A relic bestowed great power on Scarlett. A demon removed that gift. Can she summon the true fire inside and save the world? Only with her back to the wall, will this girl shine!

The Blasphemous Welcome: Dark Wen Book # 1

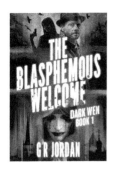

A demonic entity prepares a bloody path for its master. Four fiendish ways for the city folk to die. A cynical, battle weary detective must become his home's heavenly protector.

Join Detective Trimble and fresh faced Kyla Corstain as they enter a world of evil and ungodly manipulation causing murder, mayhem and disaster. The war for a city's soul begins now!

The Dark Wen series opens with a fanfare of destruction and death raining upon a city held in the grip of an unknown force. If you like dark powers, fast paced action and a generous dose of occult warfare, then "The Blasphemous Welcome" will satisfy your story cravings.

An explosive hello to evil incarnate!

Austerley & Kirkgordon Box Set: Books 1-3 and Origins 1-3

A retired bodyguard looking for a little fun before it's too late. An obsessive Professor, seeking the darkest things of life. And an Elder god seeking to rule the world, if they can't stop him.

Join Austerley and Kirkgordon on thr rollercoaster ride that is their first three adventures. Comprising 3 full novels as well as three accompanying origin novellettes, this collection will introduce you to a polarised duo that are the world's best hope. Joining them for the adventure are a myriad of strange characters, bizarre anmals, evil humans and the UK's finest agents from its most secret agency.

As one reviewer put it, "If you like Lovecraft, Poe, or Author Conan Doyle you will like this book. If like tv show like Buffy the Vampire Slayer, Supernatural, Being Human, or X-Files you will like this book."

So take a chance on a molotov cocktail of a duo and see how to save the world on the wild side.

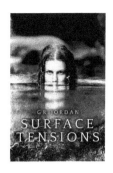

Surface Tensions: Island Adventures #1

Mermaids sighted near a Scottish island. A town exploding in anger and distrust. And Donald's got to get the sexiest fish in town, back in the water.

"Surface Tensions" is the first story in a series of Island adventures from the pen of G R Jordan. If you love comic moments, cosy adventures and light fantasy action, then you'll love these tales with a twist.

Get the book that amazon readers said, "perfectly captures life in the Scottish Hebrides" and that explores "human nature at its best and worst".

Something's stirring the water!

Lightning Source UK Ltd.
Milton Keynes UK
UKHW040608010719
345353UK00001B/4/P